THE TEN THOUSAND THINGS

Dead West Book Two

WRITTEN BY

Tim Marquitz,
J.M. Martin &
Kenny Soward

RAGNAROK PUBLICATIONS

CRESTVIEW HILLS, KENTUCKY

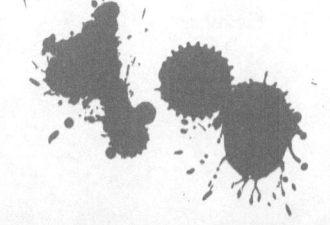

THE TEN THOUSAND THINGS (Dead West #2)
Ragnarok Publications | www.ragnarokpub.com
Editor In Chief: Tim Marquitz | Creative Director: J.M. Martin

Published by Ragnarok Publications
206 College Park Drive, Ste. 1
Crestview Hills, KY 41017

ISBN-10: 0-9913605-4-0
ISBN-13: 978-0-9913605-4-3
Worldwide Rights
Created in the United States of America

Book design: J.M Martin
Photography: AFREEMAN Photography
Cover models: Shea Dameron, Kinsey Renshaw, Dean Homsher

ACKNOWLEDGEMENTS

THE WRITERS WOULD LIKE TO THANK George Romero for the popularization of the zombie genre (and for being George Romero), Akira Kurosawa for *Yojimbo*, Sergio Leone for the "Spaghetti Western" genre and the Dollars Trilogy, and his father, Roberto Roberti, née Vincenzo Leone, for not only having Sergio, but for his pioneering 1913 film, *La Vampira Indiana* (The Indian Vampire), which is arguably the first Weird Western mash-up.

Also, thanks to Timothy W. Long for his marketing counsel and excellent cover blurb; check out Tim's military zom-poc series, *Z-Risen*.

"I AM THE SPIRIT THAT NEGATES.
AND RIGHTLY SO, FOR ALL THAT COMES TO BE
DESERVES TO PERISH WRETCHEDLY;
'TWERE BETTER NOTHING WOULD BEGIN.
THUS EVERYTHING THAT YOUR TERMS [OF],
SIN, DESTRUCTION, AND EVIL REPRESENT—
THAT IS MY PROPER ELEMENT."

— JOHANN WOLFGANG VON GOETHE, *Faust*

CHAPTER ONE

Nina Weaver dreamed in a turbulent half sleep. The sounds of gunshots and groans reached her ears, the smells of blood and death smacked her in the face. The steady thrum of anxiety resounded as *deaduns* reached out of the hellish firelight, their skinless arms glistening wet and sinewy, their maws of sharp, ivory-thick teeth snapping.

Shoshone drums echoed in the empty spaces between the undead moans and hisses. The percussive thunder drove Nina's heartbeat, bold and steady. She spun in a delicate, deadly dance, gun in one hand, hunting knife in the other. Deaduns fell, head-shot or eye-popped. Their skulls became nothing but puzzles of holes and soft spots,

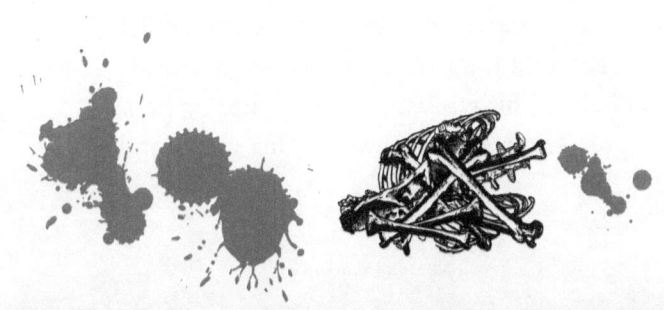

places to invade with lead and steel.

She weren't afraid here in the dream, knowing she and her *friends* had taken on the Devil himself and kicked his teeth in. In fact, there was a prevailing sense of comfort, an assuredness, in what they'd done, and a grim determination to see their way through whatever else Hell had to offer.

Beneath it all, in her dreamy, fatigue-blanketed haze, hummed the unbroken, locomotive composition of vibration and sound, the song of the iron horse, the low chug and high chitter of the *Magpie* on her wheels of steel. They swayed on the tracks of innovation, huffing and coursing through the Sierras in the pale moonlight.

Her only fear now was losing what she'd gained in such a short period of time: her first and only lover, the mysteriously exhilarating James Manning; her first female friend, a black prostitute named Jasmine; the orphaned Rachel Buell—who, at barely thirteen, had lost both her parents and her entire world—the Christianized Nez Perce tribesman called Red Thunder; and, of course, her pa, Lincoln.

Chick, chick...scratch...

Nina opened her eyes, lids still heavy with sleep.

Chick...chick...

What was that? A buffet of wind and pebble against the glass? The sound of a rodent rummaging through the nearby crates?

Nina took a deep breath through her nose. She was warm, but not uncomfortably so. Her stomach was fuller than it had been in a long time, and James Manning snuggled behind her, his tall, strong form eclipsing hers, his arm laid protectively over her waist. Nina smiled and reached out to touch her Colt 1861 Navy where it rested just inches away.

Hard iron in front, an iron-hard man behind. She was covered.

They rested on the window couch, which had been pulled out to make a bed. There were three such fold-down bunks in the train car and enough bedrolls and mats that everyone had a place to kick off their boots for a spell.

...*chick, chick, chick*...

Nina backed into Manning and nestled against his chest, stealing more of his warmth. She covered his arm with hers, running her fingers along the back of his hand, tracing her fingertips along the veins and scabbed knuckles. In the quiet half-sleep, Nina was learning the pleasures of a man's companionship, scratching the surface of love, lust, or whatever lay in between, she supposed.

They'd all come to agreeable terms for the first night on the train, hoping to be in more 'civilized' territory come morning. Even Mean George Daggett had shown some sensibilities as a human being once the train was underway, volunteering to take watch in the turret. His brother, Mason, on the other hand, snored mightily at the moment on the floor, despite Strobridge's attempts to pay him to man the engine.

Thoughts of J.H. Strobridge made Nina frown. She'd spied the revolting bastard passing some bills to Jasmine in exchange for time alone on the back deck of the gun car. The railroad boss seemed gratified to know someone still found his money worthwhile, and Jasmine, despite Strobridge having struck her not so long ago, had been unable to shed her *cocotte's* corset, taking the man's money obviously figuring it was worth the loss of another tooth.

Nina wondered if Strobridge had hidden caches of money all over the train. Probably had a wad stuffed up his shithole, too. She supposed she trusted the animals, provided they were regularly fed and watered.

...chick, chick...scratch...

The sound had become an annoyance, and she didn't think it was coming from inside the cabin. All the same, she couldn't see a damn thing through the glass, despite the pane not twelve inches from her face. It was dark inside and the muted light of the shuttered lantern swinging from the ceiling only made it more difficult. It painted the glass with faintly moving reflections.

She reckoned she could sit up and remove the shutter, take a look outside...

"You all right?" Manning whispered near her ear, his breath on her neck causing a pleasant ripple across her shoulders.

"Yeah," Nina whispered. "Just a noise." She noticed his hardness against her backside and gave a slight wiggle.

Manning's sleepy chuckle tickled her ear. "Keep that up and we're going to have issues."

The implication excited her. "I think I can deal with issues."

"Yeah. Yeah, I've noti—"

Bam!

Something slammed against the window. Nina's heart leapt. She jerked up, fully awake, causing Manning to tumble off the narrow bed. She snatched her Colt, cocked it, and pointed the barrel at the square of black glass. Manning got to one knee and grabbed his pistol belt with its holstered dragoons from the bench next to the fold-out.

Mason Daggett spoke up from over near the crates of whiskey. "Hey! How's about you lovebirds give it—"

"Shhh," Manning silenced him. "Something out there."

Mason came up quick as a shot. "What the Sam Hill you talkin' about?"

"Something just thumped the window," Nina said.

"Sure it wasn't the back of your head? The way you two—"

"Just fetch the lantern, would you?" Manning interrupted, his voice gone cold.

Mason grumbled under his breath but got up, while Jasmine and Nina shuffled over from the ass-end of the car, huddled together beneath a shared woolen blanket. Mason edged past them, handing over the lantern. Manning took it, removed the shutter, and turned the knob on the side, producing a bright orange glow.

"What is it?" Rachel asked. She looked small and quivering with the voluptuous, long-legged, dark-skinned Jasmine alongside her, the whore's arm draped around the girl's bony shoulders.

Nina looked to James. "Hold it up," she said, and he came forward to direct the light on the window. She frowned, noticing a dark splotch and a feather pasted against the glass.

Jasmine tiptoed up. "That scratchin' at the window's been going on a while."

Mason snorted. "All o' ya'll just gone and cracked. Scratchin'? Just a goddamn bird with rotten lu—"

BAM!

They all jumped—Mason included—as something

struck the glass again, this time creating a tiny hole and a spiderweb of cracks. Wind licked at the breach, train sounds leaking in.

Bam! Flap, flap! Thump! Thump!

"A whole flock slammin' into us!" Jasmine's voice rose with the increase of muffled *thumps* as more things pelted the windows.

A flutter of feathers alighted near the spot of the break, clawed feet finding purchase on the lip below the window. Wings fluttered to keep it affixed. A dark beak started pecking out small pieces of glass.

"That ain't normal," Manning said.

"What the blazes is normal since this shit started?" Mason pulled his blood-crusted trousers up over his grimy underclothes.

"They's crows," Jasmine said.

The bird pecking at the glass then stuck its head through the hole, its eyes bulging like black bubbles. Nina knew those eyes. This weren't no normal bird at all. Those were the same dark orbs she'd seen more than once in the hungry visages of certain deaduns, in the eyes of Rachel's father, Grover, when he was possessed by the yellow hooded devil, Liao Xu. It was the foul sorcerous gaze of the orchestrator of the world's end, the self-proclaimed master of Hell's own demons. It was as if Liao was looking right at them.

The bird stopped its frantic twisting, gaze flitting between those in the car. Nina gaped as the crow's beak stretched impossibly into a smile.

Yep. She was *dad gum* right. The devil had found them.

"As I thought," the bird croaked, its voice an amalgam of crow and Liao Xu. "Cowards running on the tracks, running on the line, running from death, *caw, caw!*"

"Get the priest," Nina said over her shoulder, unable to pull her gaze from the grotesque crow-thing. Jasmine nodded and hustled toward the back.

The pummeling of flying creatures against glass and side panels along the car increased to a thunderous level. How many of those awful things were outside the car? She pictured the train covered in hundreds of the wicked creatures, cawing and flapping and pecking. Pecking at anything—at *anyone*.

Rachel Buell screamed and covered her ears.

Nina turned and held up her hand. "Jasmine, wait!"

"I found you out, found you out, *caw, caw!*" the bird crowed.

"To hell with this." Manning came forward, grabbed the crow's head, and yanked it right off the creature's body. He turned to say something else, but at that moment, an explosion came from the gun car.

Mason cussed. "Georgie's in the damn turret."

"He's firing the cannon?" Nina asked.

"Well it sure as shit sounds like it, don't it?" Mason replied, snatching up his rifle.

"We gotta get to the gun car." Manning said.

"Us, too?" Jasmine grabbed Rachel's arm and pulled her close.

Nina nodded. "These devil crows are gonna break through any second."

"The gun car's armored. It's our best bet." Manning snatched a cover off their makeshift bed. "Find some blankets, throw them over your heads. Be careful crossing. One misstep and you'll end up under the train instead of on it."

"What about all those birds?" Rachel asked, breathing heavy, clinging to Jasmine, her big scared eyes even wider in the lantern's light.

Jasmine pulled her even closer. "It's gonna be all right. We'll help each other across. Okay?"

They took what they could—Mason looked at the whiskey crate, grabbed a bottle and tucked it in a leather satchel, then another, and put the satchel over his shoulder—then they formed up at the back of the car.

Crows pelted the windows, leaving bloody smears on the glass. *Thump, thump, thump,* the rhythm of wet meat slapping against the train grew frantic. Suddenly a window shattered and a frenzy of black shadows poured in.

"Now!" Nina shouted, anxious to be away from the maniacal crows, pushing the others forward as panic gnawed at her edges.

Manning slid the cabin door open and leapt across the dark divide. He made it across, took a second to position himself, then threw open the door to the gun car. Mason hung the lantern on an outside hook and followed Manning over, then the two men stood on either side of brink, arms out, waiting to receive Rachel, who held her dingy gray blanket over her head, hesitated, looked at Jasmine and then at Nina.

"C'mon!" Mason hollered, the bouncing lantern light twisting his features.

"Jump, Rachel," yelled Manning over the wind and the coming tide of deranged crows. "We got you. Look at me! Jump right across to us!"

Vague shadows emerged from the night as the girl cried

out and leapt, beaks and claws grabbing at her coverlet. Mason batted at them as Manning pulled the girl to safety. Rachel clutched onto him and buried her face in his chest, the crows in a tumult all around. No time for coddling, Manning pushed the girl inside the gun car.

Nina ducked as a flurry of feathers blew by from behind, flying out of the train car from within. One rammed her shoulder, and she gave a backhanded swing with her knife. The bird-thing shrieked more than cawed.

Nina fought every instinct to shove Jasmine out of her way, but the woman stood at the precipice, struggling to get the cover over her head, the wind and cawing creatures whipping and pulling at it. Already leaning into her jump, Jasmine likely couldn't see a blamed thing.

Nina yelled at her, heart thumping in her chest, picturing her friend tumbling through the gap to an awful demise. Instead Jasmine let go of the cowl, surrendering it to the crows, yelled something that was lost in the sounds of engine and wind and beast, and leapt. She barely made it across, her already-torn dress snagging on the swaying coupler pin between the cars. Mason grabbed her flailing arm and pulled her away from the edge, leaving a long strip of petticoat fluttering from the connector.

Another solid mass of feathers and claws dug through the back of Nina's shirt. A sharp pain jabbed between her shoulder blades. She cried out and spun, throwing herself against the car wall. The thing clutched harder, shrieking.

Nina took two steps forward, then leapt backwards, feeling the bird's hollow bones crackle beneath her weight. It squawked as she smashed it repeatedly, yet still the broken thing scratched its way up her shoulders, pecked at her head, its beak piercing flesh and thudding against the bone of her skull.

"Ow!" Nina reached back, grabbed hold of its neck, throttling it. She beat the bedamned devil crow 'gainst the train over and over. More of them flapped and cawed wildly around her.

"Nina!"

The shout seemed to come from miles away, little more than a whisper. Her eyes fixed on a beast of a bird as it came, wings thrown wide, head jerking around, needle beak seeking her flesh. Another swooped across the cabin and banked in her direction.

Infernal no-good goddamn peck of trouble, Nina thought with a flash of sardonic macabre, then turned, took a couple running steps, and leapt. The gun car rushed to meet her during a long moment of weightlessness, then she fell into Manning's arms. Mason reached out to steady them both.

"Thanks," she said to Manning, then to Mason. "You, too."

Mason backed toward the gun car's open doorway. "I know ya'll think I'm some no-count tinhorn shitlicker, but we Alabama boys got guts, and we don't leave our own…" he turned to duck inside the gun car, then looked at Manning and Nina both, "…even if you're a high falutin' Blue Belly and one of your heathen fuckin' kind."

Nina appreciated his conviction, but frowned at being called a heathen. She was about to toss something back, but Manning spoke first, saying, "I told you before, I'm not a Yankee."

"Ya are to me," Mason said over his shoulder, ducking inside the gun car.

Manning had his arm around Nina's shoulders. "Why does he keep calling me a Yankee?"

"Maybe it's your mustache," she said, and pulled him inside along behind her.

"What?" He slid the door shut behind them.

Nina didn't answer, instead she started checking herself for wounds.

"You okay?" he asked.

"I dunno. My hat…" She'd left it behind. The thought vexed her.

Manning nodded. A man like him understood the importance of a good Stetson. "Well, least we're breathing. Hat or not, we still got that much."

"I just ain't so sure I like this new *haircut*." A crooked smile stretched her lips at the thought of her butchered hair. Hell of a time to worry about that. She'd been around James Manning two days and was already feeling vain about her looks.

Manning brushed a short lock behind her ear. "Look more than fine to me, Nina girl. Now what did you mean about my mustache?"

"What in Tarnation is going on?" said Pa from one of the bunks, his hair still wild from sleep. "George up top seems to have finally cracked his nut."

Strobridge was in the bunk next to Pa's, mumbling and pulling on his boots. Jasmine and Rachel were cleaving to one another again, while Father Mathias, as alert as someone could be just shook awake by cannon fire, hung a lantern from a ceiling hook.

"Hey, Injun, don't touch my brother," Mason said, making his way to the turret. "Go on. Get."

Red Thunder had been beneath the turret, gazing up at George. The Indian turned his head and gave Mason a dark look. He refused to move, and Pa hobbled between them, still in his long undergarments. "Now ain't the time to crawl humps, fellas," he said, facing Mason, his back to Red Thunder—Nina noticed his placement with a tiny spate of pride.

At the same time, she touched the surge of pain at the base of her neck, drew her fingers back wet with blood. "Crows attacked our car, came in through the windows—"

Another *boom* shook the train. The vibration rattled Nina's skull. She put her pinky in her ear and itched as the acrid stink of black powder infiltrated the cabin.

"Take that, you *sumbitch*," George hollered from the turret.

Mason called up to his brother. "What the Sam Hill you doin' up there, Georgie?"

Nina could make out the passing coal clouds around the turret cage and George's sweaty face. His eyes were crazed, fixed on something behind them. His fear was contagious, and Nina was catching it. She glanced at the cabin door, which led to the porch where she'd recently kissed Manning for the first time.

"I'm takin' out the fuckin' tracks!"

"Why the hell you doing that?" Mason asked his brother.

"So it *cain't* follow!"

Folks looked at one another, then Pa shouted up, "So *what* can't follow?"

"Christ Almighty, ya'll blind?" George glanced down, and then pointed somewhere behind the train. "*That!*"

Everyone in the car but Pa bolted for the rear door.

They gathered on the porch. Nina's view was blocked at first but the curses and stiffening backs made her squeeze between Red Thunder and Strobridge to see what the fuss was about. She instantly wished she hadn't.

They were on the decline well beyond Summit, and a growling iron beast careened down the mountain behind them, devouring track by the yard, plowing wakes of billowing smoke into the crow-infested sky. The engine was an immense, charcoal-colored cylinder; it seemed twice the size of Strobridge's *Magpie*. Its cyclopean lamp bathed the tracks in a crimson glow, sniffing the path like a hellhound hot to scent.

"Christ Almighty indeed," said Strobridge low, but right next to Nina.

"Not Christ, Mister Strobridge," said Father Mathias from behind them. "Liao."

"George has the right idea, but he ain't got the angle," Manning said, then turned to Red Thunder. "We got anything that will bust these tracks up?"

Red Thunder stared at the hellish engine and shrugged. "Maybe."

An image of the cackling Lester Woodruff tossing his explosives flashed in Nina's mind, then another image of the beaten man's battered face and that revolver in his hand. *Her* revolver. '*Lee me uh-wone*,' he'd said through broken teeth. The man's last words. She swallowed and forced the thought away.

Pa pushed in behind her, steadying himself on her shoulder as he gazed at the furious machine bearing down the mountain. "You don't see that every day."

A squall came from the sky as a mass of feathered beak-

and-claw shadows dove on them, a thousand or more of the black devil crows.

Before anyone could retreat inside, Father Mathias produced a rosary of brown and marbled beads from his pocket, its chain encircled his fist, and he dangled the image of his Christ god on a silver cross; she remembered Pa calling it a Crucifix. Wound about his hand, too, was the golden key Nina recognized as the Taiping Jing, the very object Liao Xu was after.

"Hold fast! All things of nature are of God and by God," the priest implored everyone, then leaned forward against the rail and glared at the undulating flock. "You are compelled by demonic forces," Father Mathias yelled. "Hear me! You are not at fault. Turn away! Turn away from the path of the damned—"

Just as the swarm reached them—Nina felt the noise of their descent like a buzzing in her ears—the priest raised the key and Crucifix high, shouting at the top of his lungs, looking the part of some avenging saint with the tails of his black robes flapping. "God, hear my prayer, hearken to the words of my mouth, for I am your most unworthy minister who trusts in you. Lord, you are my strength. You are my tower and my shield! In the name of the Holy Mother, Virgin of virgins, and all holy angels and archangels and orders of blessed spirits, deliver us, O Lord, from all evil. Deliver us from the snares of the devil, from anger, from hatred, from all ill will! Depart, you devils! Begone, you hostile powers!"

The birds broke from their deadly formation, cawing as they flew away, now seemingly unburdened by Liao Xu's magic. The demon train's howls echoed off the sides of the mountains as the birds vanished into night sky.

Pa patted Mathias on the back. "Good work, Father."

Mathias smiled and pointed up. "Glory be," he said.

"Okay, Father, okay," Pa laughed. "Due credit to the Almighty."

"Amen, brother." Mathias tucked the rosary inside his robe.

Strobridge gripped the rail, head cocked sideways. "What in the blazes is this? We're speeding up."

"Good," said Nina.

"Not necessarily."

Pa glanced about, his eyes like darting squirrels in the sunken pits of their sockets. "Buck's manning the engine. He know what he's doing?"

"That thing behind us might have spooked him and he turned up the heat." Strobridge pushed his hair back against his head in a smoothing motion. "The next several miles is mostly a straight run, but we'll be hitting some winding track directly, and that ain't no place to run this engine full out. Besides, keep this up and the fool will blow the goddamn boiler while he's at it. I shoulda stayed up there."

Manning leaned against the rail, glaring at the monstrosity gaining ground on them. Nina could almost see the man's wheels turning, trying to find an answer. He turned. "Me, Mason, and Strobridge will head up front. The rest of you," he nodded up the tracks, "what can we do about that?"

"Keep shootin'," Mason said.

"Well, George can shoot to his heart's delight," Manning said, "and maybe he'll get lucky, but I say we check what we got by way of explosives. Maybe we can get that monster derailed. You with me, Red?"

The Indian nodded and they went inside the car, Manning giving Nina's arm a squeeze as he passed by.

"I'll help," her pa said, hobbling inside after them.

Nina watched, feeling useless, then gazed back at the red-hot cinder following them down the tracks. "How long you think we got?"

Father Mathias clutched her shoulder, the same spot Manning had just touched. "Nina, I need you to do something for me."

"Yeah? And what'd that be?" After that display, turning away the devil crows, Nina had just put a great deal more faith in this man of God.

"I need you to procure a bit of coal," he said.

CHAPTER TWO

KEEP SHOOTING, GEORGE," MASON called up to his brother from beneath the turret.

"Yes, sir." George's voice was determined, if a touch panicky, no doubt falling back on his soldierly training. He shouted something incomprehensible, and Nina saw Mason slap his hands over his ears. The rest followed suit just as the cannon went off. The air swam with discharge, and Nina stifled a sneeze, her eyes watering.

Manning took her arm. "Did he say why?"

She'd told James that she was coming with them, that Father Mathias needed some of those black bricks from the hopper. "You noticed well as me he don't elaborate

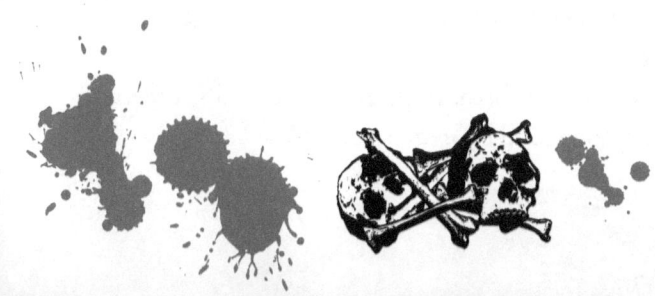

much with the details unless he's spouting off about the Lord and what-not."

Manning looked at the priest as he entered the car. "Yeah."

"More fuckin' birds!" George hollered down, his voice a couple octaves higher than usual.

"I thought you got rid of 'em all." Strobridge growled, looking crossways at Father Mathias.

"I freed as many as the Almighty deemed worthy. Perhaps Liao turned some back toward us."

Maybe the Black Robe's God had second thoughts about delivering them from the devil's snare after all.

"That's just capital," Strobridge glowered. "Well, come on, gents. No sense in wasting any more time."

Manning squeezed Nina's arm. "You sure you want to do this?"

She gave him a look, pulled her arm away. "I'll be fine."

Passing by, Mason grinned. "We'll go up first, then you come up. Maybe we can draw them birds to us and give you a better chance of keepin' your pretty Injun eyes from gettin' plucked out."

"Y'all just watch out for yourselves," she tossed back at him. What did these men think she and Pa had been doing all these years on their own? Picking daisies?

"Let's go," said Strobridge. Irritation—or fear, more like—lent an even more severe edge to his voice. Hers as well, she figured.

"Careful, Nina girl," Pa said, hobbling over to give her a quick hug.

"Lord have mercy," Strobridge grumbled and shuffled his boots. Mason stood by, expressionless.

"Keep your damn hat on." Manning looked square at the railroad boss. "Quit trying to superintend everything."

"Let's just get this shit done and over," Mason said and slid the door open. He shouldered by Strobridge and sprang across to the other car. The railroad boss jumped next, as smooth as if he'd done it a thousand times before—which he probably had—then Manning, and finally Nina, after giving Pa a peck on his hairy cheek and assuring him she'd be okay.

The luxury car was occupied by at least a dozen of the raucous devil crows that hadn't escaped, and Nina saw Strobridge kick one broke-winged bird away in an explosion of feathers.

One of them sprang at her from the oak table, cawing and flapping. She raised a protective hand in front of her face, remembering Mason's jibe about her eyes, and roundhoused the monstrous bird. It hit the ground and was still, and right near her hat, too! It looked a little the worse for wear, but better than the dead bird. She grabbed it up, put it on her head, and shinned it to the far end of the car, with more of the crowing bastards going mad all around her. She ran out on the small deck, the damned black devils beating on her back, and Manning shut the door hard behind her with an echoing *thud*. The birds that made it out with her gave up the fight, flying off into the night, cawing and screeching.

"Hey." Manning's grin was lit by Strobridge's lamp. "Got your hat back."

He gave a good-natured nod as if they hadn't just run a gauntlet of claws and bird shit, and she found she appreciated the man even more, despite his protective urges chafing her a bit. Manning meant well, and she was thankful for it. Her and Pa owed him their lives, from the scrape back in Coburn—or Truckee or crispy-deadun-shitville or whatever the hell it was called now—as well as his assistance getting to the fort, not to mention for him standing firm with 'em against Strobridge and the Daggetts.

"Let's go," he said.

The tender car ladder stared them in the face. Mason leaped first, grabbing the ladder and clambering up. Nina looked down and noticed the dark blur of tracks sliding by faster than before. The squawks of crows seemed to have fiercely died down, perhaps due to Father Mathias's holy magic, or the gaining speed of the train; Nina didn't know which, and didn't much care.

"When I get across," Manning said, leaning in, "take my hand and I'll pull you over." Before she could protest, he leapt across the divide, foregoing the tender car platform, caught the ladder, then put his arm out to her.

"Or you could just do this," said Strobridge. He stepped across to the deck, switched his lamp to the other hand, mashed his hat down on his greasy head, and turned expertly up the rungs. The man had obviously been born to ride the rail. Nina looked at James and James looked at Strobridge. The boss chuckled at Manning, and they both hung the rails facing one another. James dropped his extended arm and started up, Strobridge just behind him. Nina opted for the boss man's maneuver.

A lazy, half-moon had wandered out from behind the clouds, bathing the tender car in halfway decent light. Mason and Manning were most of the way across already, covering up to avoid crow attacks. The birds hadn't noticed her and Strobridge, and the man passed over to a large slab of steel with rungs in the top, motioning for Nina to join him.

"I had this put on to make crossing to the engine easier."

Nina nodded, figuring the railroad boss knew what he was doing. The wind blew her hat back, and she pushed it down on her head.

"Grab that other rung there and lift. It's heavy as hell."

Nina did, and together they lifted the steel door, its hinges squeaking, and slammed it over. With only a couple feet to maneuver around the edges now, and the ground whizzing by below, Nina felt a surge of panic. She was on her guard, this close to Strobridge, alone and vulnerable, him with every advantage. Her hand brushed her holster, felt the reassuring grip of her six-shooter.

Strobridge didn't let on if he noticed her touching her iron. "There you go," he said. "All the coal you need. Although, gotta admit, hard to tell what use it will be to that holier-than-thou Bible thumpin' bastard." He didn't wait for her to say anything, just climbed down the short ladder and into the engine's cab. Nina wanted to know what was happening down there, but she couldn't dwell on it. Crow call filled the night.

The coal chamber was nearly chock-full, so she spread the rolled blanket she'd brought on the top of the car and hopped in. After stabilizing herself on the mound, she placed black nuggets on the blanket one-by-one. She watched warily as the black birds wheeled nearer, and while she couldn't see it, she could *feel* coal grit everywhere—in her nose, her lungs, probably in the crack of her ass, too.

She gathered as much as she thought she could carry,

figuring better to have too much than not enough, then pulled the ends of the blanket together and lifted the bundle to her waist. After just a few feet of scuffling, she realized she'd not fully appreciated the totality of her burden. She grumbled a curse beneath her breath and set the coal down on top of the tender car.

Nina glanced at her surroundings, looking for the damned birds, and noticed right away they must have come to one of the high trestle bridges that she and Pa had both admired on occasion as a work of art. "There just ain't no tellin' what man can do all together and with the proper motivation to shape somethin' instead of destroy it," Pa had marveled once as they stared up from down in a gulch at the orderly mess of clean-hewn timbre and steel spanning cliff-face to cliff-face.

Now she had a view from the topside, the land all around done gone away, dropped off into oblivion as far as her eyes could see. Shadowy hills loomed in the distance. Rough treetops swayed far, far below. A wisp of cloud passed by overhead.

They were riding the sky.

Nina's legs weakened. She collapsed to one knee, head spinning because of the dizzying height. The vibrating roof offered no relief; in fact, it threatened to shake her off. She raised her eyes to the fiery locomotive coming down the mountain behind them. Its menace remained. A terrifying, oppressive weight. What could Father Mathias do with an infernal sack of coal? She should leave it and get her ass back inside.

The cannon exploded again. Nina squeezed her eyes shut. "Shit."

What if blowing up the tracks didn't work? She didn't know what Father Mathias wanted with the coal, but she told him she'd fetch it, so fetch it she would. "Help me, *boha gande.*"

The rumble came, the first indication the People were near...*bum-bum-ta-ta, bum-bum-ta-ta...*

Nina clutched the sound to her heart, willing it louder in her head, pulling the song of the Shoshone out of the dream space like water from a well. It was a soft pattern, accentuated by rising voices.

She looked up, determination flooding her body...*bum-bum-ta-ta, bum-bum-ta-ta...*

Nina clutched the bundle of coal with both hands and focused on the end of the tender car. Just another fifteen, maybe twenty feet. She could make it.

...*bum-bum-ta-ta, bum-bum-ta-ta...BOOM!*

The final, emphatic beat thrust Nina to her feet and shoved her forward. Her knees bumped against her awkward bundle as she stumbled to the edge of the tender car.

Suddenly a cluster of crazed crows slammed into her from behind, ripping and cawing, trying to tear off her head. She mashed her hat back down as they pecked and clawed away at her.

Nina made a bestial noise as she punched at a bird. Her makeshift sack slipped from her grip. She recovered, clutching the twisted end with two hands again, but too late. The weight caused her to lean out over the emptiness with nothing to bring her back. She was going down.

Nina gritted her teeth, feeling them grind together. There was only one way to keep from falling head first into the abyss…

She leapt, taking burden and birds with her, hoping to reach the luxury car's deck but sure she'd end up cut to pieces beneath the train before tumbling into the breach below. Her stomach violently reversed direction as she landed on the coal bundle, air bursting from her lungs and chest exploding in pain. She wanted to draw a breath, but nothing worked. The only sensation was razor beaks and beating wings making hay on her head and neck.

Nina lunged, pinned one between the top of her skull and the luxury car's door. Wings buffeted her. Blackness formed at the edge of her vision; yet, a red hot fire burned inside, fueling her body to work, driving away the darkness.

Nina butted the devil crow again, felt the dislocating crunch of the bird's insides. She took it by the neck and hurled the dying thing between the cars, cutting short its caws. Another drove its beak into the meat of her left arm and Nina yelped in pain.

The car door swung open and Nina heard Pa bellow. "Hyah!"

A thump, then another, and all the cawing and fluttering stopped.

"Nina," Pa grabbed her arm and started to pull her up.

"Wait," she managed to spit, just before her stomach heaved and she vomited peaches and dried beef across the deck.

Through shallow breaths and sting-watery eyes, Nina listened to the *Magpie* chug along, waiting for her body to re-balance. She closed her eyes, wishing she could wind back time as easily as a watch when she and Manning had been curled up together. But Liao Xu's relentless pursuit had begun once again, driving death like a plow through a field.

Jasmine's voice floated above the clank and chug of rails and engine. "Here. I'll help."

They lifted Nina to her feet and ushered her into the car. Inside, a few dead crows were here and there, the rest gone, the far door open.

Nina accepted a quick hug from Pa and Jasmine, then said "The coal…"

Jasmine nodded. "I'll get it."

"Thanks." Nina's shoulders slumped as she worked to catch her breath, feeling grateful for just a moment's rest, but worried all the same.

"You okay?" Pa asked.

She nodded, and her father squeezed her shoulder, leaving his hand there while Jasmine carried the coal across the cabin. Pa sat her on the lip of the bed where she and Manning had been snuggled warm and safe not so long ago.

"Catch your breath, Nina girl. You done good." He gave her shoulder a last rub then limped off toward the far end of the car.

Nina pulled her hat off and looked at it. The thing was as beaten and full of holes as she felt. She laid it down beside her and tried to still her mind for a bit.

Something tugged on her shirt and she opened her eyes, not realizing she'd had them shut. Rachel Buell held out a damp rag. Nina took a long look at the girl. Wide-set eyes sat above a long, straight nose. She was pretty. Spitting image of her mother, Clara, who'd died gruesomely—but died *fighting*.

Nina nodded. "Thank you."

The girl returned the nod. Nina wondered at the overwhelming sadness, confusion, and anger that would come to her later, out of the clear blue, when the full weight of losing both parents would hit like a rock to the head. She wanted to hug Rachel, but what had any of Pa's hugs done for her after her own mother's death?

Only prove you were loved, she thought. *That someone actually cared.*

Nina started to reached for Rachel, but she'd already turned away, pulling up her torn skirts and sticking fast to Jasmine's heels as though she were the black prostitute's shadow. Nina regretted the missed opportunity, then wiped the rag across her stinging neck. She needed to stop thinking of Jasmine as some mere soiled dove. The woman had proven to be much more than that.

She scrubbed at her neck a tad vigorously. She was damn annoyed with Liao Xu; that much was sure, and she decided it wasn't yet time to take it easy. She tossed the dirt-soiled rag on the bed, took up her hat, and followed them to the armored car.

Inside, she stopped near the gun turret to look at George Daggett's dirt-crusted boots, then glanced up at the scalawag. Even in the wan light she could see his screw-mouth curl beneath his brambly mustache, as well as the lump on his cheek from Manning having laid into him back in the tunnels beneath Fort Bluff. George looked down at her, but there was no mistaking the distant stare that seemed to look someplace beyond—beyond her, beyond everything.

"Like fuckin' Cumberland. We's fuckin' biting bullets from Billy Yank all day. They kept comin' at us and comin'..."

He chuckled, face smoothing as he made a connection. "Mahone wasn't about to give up that hill, though. Hell no. He said, 'Today we stand...today we stand.' So we dug in round this big regal church. Mase, he was off on one of his special missions, so the fellers started looking to me. Goddamn, that was some fightin'. Hey, you think the Black Robe, you think maybe he's our church?"

"What?" Nina wasn't quite following George's rambling.

"The priest. Mathias. Maybe we need to dig in 'round him and fight these bastards off."

"Might be something to that." Then Nina headed out to the back deck and the rear of the train where Father Mathias and Pa watched Red Thunder string together some salvaged blast balls made by the erstwhile Lester "Woodie" Woodruff. She noted how he was braiding the wicks all together, reminding her of a makeshift *boleadoras* like gauchos used when running cattle.

The priest looked over as she stepped onto the deck. "And not without some small sacrifice, it seems," he said.

"I reckon I got pecked a bit. What's going on here?"

"Lincoln tells us there's another bridge coming up. We're going to remove the option of pursuit for Liao Xu's monstrosity."

"Gonna blow it up," Pa said, shrugging on a threadbare, bloodstained overcoat.

Nina glared up the tracks at said monstrosity. It had taken the straightaway like an iron stallion, pistons and rods churning in frantic rage, billowing exhaust like a dark cape, blacker than night. It couldn't be more than a couple miles distant, maybe less. "How long you think we've got?"

"We'll get our chance well before that thing gets to us."

Pa's foot had taken to healing well, and he was mobile enough, able to put a decent amount of weight on it. According to Pa and Father Mathias—neither of them doctors—it wasn't broken. "I've had a heap worse than this. Just came at a wretched time is all," Pa had told her once they'd boarded the train and had a chance to look everyone over. Still, she hated to see him traipsing around on it, acting like it was right as rain.

"Why don't you get inside, Pa. Give your foot a rest?"

"My foot is right as rain, thank you."

"Then at least sit down."

"Your daughter's right, Lincoln," Mathias said. "No need to push yourself. 'I pray that all may go well with you, and that you may be in good health, as it goes well with your soul.' The Book of John."

"Never could argufy the words of the Evangelist," her pa said, but she could tell it was grousingly, though he hid it well enough.

Jasmine retrieved a folded blanket from one of the bunks, and Pa sat against the door frame, removed his boot and rested his foot on it. To Nina it still looked god-awful.

Red Thunder sat on the deck cross-legged and seemed to meditate, and everyone was quiet for a spell. Jasmine and Rachel sat just on the other side of the car door, while the priest and Pa quietly watched the pursuing train. Nina couldn't take her eyes off the murderous thing, either. Just the sight of it filled her heart with dread. She turned and put her back to the railing.

"Up yonder near side is Dog Hill Summit," Pa said, breaking the silence and cocking his head northwards at the dark outline of a mountain. "At the rate we're going, should be about twenty-some-odd-minutes till we hit the next bridge. Made a couple runs up and down Dutch Flat when the rail line was just gathering wool."

"I take it you've been around the Sierra a long while?" Mathias asked.

"Oh, yes. Yes, I have, all the way up through Fur Country. After my long engagement with the HBC I was what they called an *avant courier*."

"We call your kind 'dog face,'" Red Thunder said without opening his eyes.

"I've heard that a time or two. Better than being called 'dog meat,' I suppose."

"Why dog face?" Jasmine asked, leaning through the doorway.

Pa smiled at her and ran his fingers through his scruffy brown and gray beard.

"Can we outrun it?" Nina asked. "Liao's train?"

"Well...we'll need to slow down near Crystal Peak. Strobridge has to know that. If we can't derail Liao, that's where he'll catch us."

Nina crossed her arms, resisting the urge to turn and look.

Mathias raised his hands, still regal even with his sprung collar and mess of chestnut hair flung out like an exploded cactus. "Have faith, good people. Believe that this will work. Nina's expedition into the coal mound will not have been in vain."

"I'd love that to be true, Father," said Pa.

"It *can* be true." Mathias took the gilded key from his coat pocket and rubbed it between his thumb and index finger.

Red Thunder opened his eyes and looked over, but it was Jasmine, still sitting just inside the armored car's threshold, who spoke up. "What does that open?"

"I've heard some of you refer to this as the Taiping Jing. You would be mistaken; however, it *does* open the Taiping Jing's reliquary…well, a small vault actually in Lake's Crossing."

"They renamed that place," said Pa.

"Indeed, after the hero of the Mexican War, the gallant soldier's soldier, General Reno. I studied his exploits at the Battle for Mexico City and also Chapultepec—"

"Sorry, Father," Pa interrupted. "You can indulge us with a history lesson later. I thought Strobridge was supposed to give you the Taiping Jing, not some key."

"That's the deal I heard," Nina added.

"That's correct, but deals are often fleeting things, hardly fair, stretched thin by time and circumstance. I was happy to at least procure this." He waved the key, lantern light glinting off its surface.

The nightmare train blew its hellish whistle, and drew Nina's eyes from the key. Her mouth went dry, and she patted her head and neck to keep her hands busy. On a more practical note, the birds had done less damage than she thought. Lots of nicks and cuts—her scalp was sore to the touch in spots—but she'd live.

"Was it the cross or the key that chased off them birds?" Nina said, confused. "I mean, if that ain't the Taiping Jing—"

"This is simply an *instrument* of the Taiping Jing, a linked artifact, if you will, with considerable power of its own. Both this key and the Taiping Jing are tools of peace and balance, forever linked."

"Peace? So, why is Liao Xu dead set on them? What can he do with 'em?"

Father Mathias raised his finger. "He can do absolutely nothing *with* them, but as long as someone with great faith and a good heart wields the relics, Liao can be countered. That is the heart of his desire for the Taiping Jing. Were he to possess it, he would be unstoppable."

The whistle blew at them again; a high, plaintive *wooo...WOO...wooo* that trailed off in hot frustration. This time they all turned. The nightmare train chugged beneath the uncovered moonlight, rounding a bend and charging between two hills, red furnace glow beneath as though it ran on the fires of Hell itself. Nina swore the cylindrical body and frame twisted on the tracks, bulging, as if something inside strained against its mechanical confines.

Rachel stepped out onto the deck, wearing one of the woolen Army blankets around her shoulders. Her long hair whipped into her face. "What's it gonna do when it catches up?" she whispered, staring.

Father Mathias shrugged. "If we are caught, all you can do is pray, little sister. Liao Xu is known for his excessive cruelty."

Rachel swallowed hard, the sound audible despite the noise.

The priest bestowed an awkward smile. "It may not console you much, but I'm certain he'll save the worst for me."

Jasmine cut in, "I think we all prefer it when you tell us to have faith."

They spent the next few minutes in silence, each one

lost in their own musing, when the *Magpie* whistled three fat *blats*, as if taunting the oncoming juggernaut. Mathias chuckled as the sound of their running changed to a high-pitched hum. Land fell away and the pre-dawn glow off the horizon left them gazing out over a valley floor covered with trees. Even safely on the crowded deck, shoulder-to-shoulder with the others, Nina went cold. She'd never been keen on heights and pretty much shied away from the taller climbs her father fearlessly traversed. She took a step back and bumped into her pa as he stood up. He put a hand on her shoulder to steady himself.

"Here we go," he said, pulling on his boot, then he nodded toward the bridge. "Time to blow these tracks. Clear the deck, folks." He gave Nina's shoulder a pat and hitched his head toward the inside of the car.

Red Thunder lifted the blast balls, mindful not to crack their clay skins against the metal guardrail. Without Woodie, no one knew how volatile his concoctions were, although Nina kind of wondered what it mattered if Red was going to toss them on the rails anyway. Still, she took a deep breath and moved back, following Jasmine and Rachel back inside the car. There was nothing left to do but trust things would work.

She sat down between Rachel and Jasmine, not wanting to engage George up in the turret again despite him yelling down if they were gonna blow the damn bridge or not. She ignored him. Talking to George Daggett made her feel more like to clout him in the beezer than have a conversation with his ornery ass.

She stared through the open door at the cluster of men on the deck, watched as Father Mathias lit the wick. Pa hobbled inside the car to join them. "You might want to back up."

They all scooted, sticking fingers in their ears. Jasmine and Rachel both closed their eyes, but Nina couldn't resist watching. Red Thunder hung out over the rail and lowered the delicate contraption of clay-shell explosives. In a swooping motion, he tossed them high and hit the deck.

Nina rose up just in time to see the balls bounce, roll, and swing between the tracks before they shattered and went off. The train rumbled and shuddered. Pa yanked Nina down and a piece of shrapnel whizzed through the door, *pinging* off the wall behind her.

"I taught you better than that!" he grit his teeth at her.

"Sorry, Pa."

After the explosions died down, they filed out to the deck to check the damage. Red Thunder and Father Mathias rolled over, watching pieces of bridge dangle and fall away into the darkness below. A huge section swayed and tumbled down, leaving an immense gap in the ties.

No way could a train pass over that.

They'd beaten Liao Xu a second time! But the relief that washed over Nina was short-lived. The bridge shuddered, and then again for good measure, threatening to shrug the *Magpie* off its iron-laden shoulders, as well.

Nina exchanged a terrified look with Jasmine. The tracks leaned slightly one way, then worked back the other, implying the possibility of a sickening free fall, before settling back into its wooden frame. They rolled onto solid land again with a shudder, and Nina breathed a sigh of relief.

"Yeah!" Pa shouted, pumping his fist in the air.

Jasmine joined him with a whoop of her own while Nina helped Father Mathias up and received a brief hug and some words in her ear. "A little faith, my daughter."

"George," Pa called. "Go tell those fellas up front we did it. Tell 'em they can set a proper speed."

Nina expected some kind of retort, but George just dropped down the short ladder, whooped "hot damn," and hurried through the train car door.

"What now?" Rachel asked.

"Now we wait."

Nina stood at the doorway, watching behind them and counting the moments as they made their getaway through the early morning hours. They rounded a shallow bend and took a path between two walls of solid granite. The sun was aching to poke its head up, and the dawning hues of copper and lavender bathed the high rock in subdued shafts of shadow and soft light.

Her stomach rumbled, but she closed her eyes and took a deep breath of the mountain air, ruined somewhat by the tinge of smoke and steel. She imagined James covered in coal dust by now, sweating dirty trickles down his lean body. It was a sad fact they'd only had a few hours to spend together. She knew exactly what she wanted to do with James Manning given a half hour more of privacy—and reckoned he felt the same way, given his *stiff* posture during their brief respite.

Another belly grumble interrupted the thought, and her mind wandered away and found instead a lump of fear in her breast. She wanted to believe they'd escaped Liao by destroying the tracks, but her gut told her something else for some reason, chasing away any last trace of pleasant thoughts. While everyone else had come inside to feel all lighthearted and victorious, she looked at Red Thunder's back and his whipping hair as he stayed at the rail, looking behind them as if he suspected the same.

"What if it somehow made it across?" Nina asked.

The Nez Perce answered after a short pause. "A dark spirit that powerful…"

Pa came up behind her. He cast a worried glance up the tracks. "We've seen some strange things lately and that's a fact. I hope you're both wrong."

Father Mathias had been sitting on a sideboard bench, leaning forward with his rosary in his hands. He looked up, his eyes dark and serious. "In addition to being excessively cruel, Liao is also exceedingly crafty."

"Best not count our chickens then," said Pa.

"How long have you known him?" Rachel's eyes were wide with wonder, asking a question Nina figured had been on everyone's mind. What precisely was the account between these two mystery men who could work miracles both astonishing and villainous?

Father Mathias lowered his head, and a shock of hair fell over his eyes. "We go back well before you were born, young lady. I'm told Liao Xu came out of nowhere, a spot of darkness that took our order by storm. He murdered three of my brethren before a formidable defense could be mounted. He was so very good with fire *and* light. An attempt to recruit him was made. The offerer was found hanged upside down from Palmer's Cross on the slopes of El Ávila, disemboweled, his abdomen splayed open, his male organ in his own…" The Black Robe priest looked at the floor with a weak smile. "That was in the Year of our

Lord Sixteen Hundred and Sixty-Seven."

Rachel gulped. Jasmine looked horrified. Pa's eyes narrowed in either disbelief or disgust, Nina wasn't certain.

She had no idea where in Tarnation that was, but her mind grasped at the date, unable to imagine the truth of such a span of time. "You're telling us that loony bastard is over two hundred years old?"

"I am telling you that."

Everyone remained silent after that, waiting for the big train to appear—or not. Nina kept her eyes on the mountainous gap as it grew more distant. Their engine had slowed noticeably as they entered a long, slow bend.

Funny how she'd gotten used to the locomotive's mannerism in the short time they'd been aboard. The sounds beneath the whistles and chugs: the throttle valve and cylinders, the running gear, the brakes, all working in steam-compressed conjunction to keep their iron horsey on the rails. And even more of a demonstration now that Strobridge was furiously working her. She flashed to a memory of his thrusting hips and grinning face as he plowed away at Jasmine's derrière back in the well room at Fort Bluff.

Nina forced the unpleasant thought away, looking at a low tangle of dense forest and brush as it ran north-eastward, breaking away from the Truckee River.

"Crystal Peak," Pa said, nodding toward the mountain.

Nina and Father Mathias followed that nod as her pa continued, "We're good and deep into Desolation Country. We'll cross under Crystal Range," he swept his left arm out, "and the Truckee passes above, to the north, meets again just east of the peaks there. And then we're bound for Reno. I figure we hold out another hour or two, should be free and clear."

Free and clear. What did that mean? Nina couldn't remember ever being free and clear. They'd been on the trail almost her entire life, and donning her boyish appearance was like putting on a second skin, all for the benefit of the town folk, as she and Pa traded possibles, usually fur and *ponche*—the stuff whites called *baccy*—for hollow woods of firewater and, in recent years, guns. Pa used to refuse to arm the native folk, but he'd changed his mind of late and she knew not to push him for his reckoning. She wondered how folks would treat them if they knew. Nina never questioned things, not too much. She didn't mind hiding what she was when she was younger. It was a game. But now she was a woman and it was harder to mask her womanliness, especially in the dry season or indoors when questions kept coming, and it stuck in her craw having to deny her breeding. Still, it was the safe thing to do, what with the Paiute and Snake People putting on black faces against the ongoing surge of settlers. Nina grinned. Hell, only good thing about this ado about the end of the world is they were all equals now purty much. Wouldn't George and Mason bust a gear to think something like that?

Not surprising, yet still to her dismay, the enemy train shot from the granite gap in a blaze of smoke and fire. Just a mile distant now, its triumphant...*woooooo...WOOO!*... pierced Nina's ears and jolted her upright.

"Oh my God," Jasmine whispered.

They all rushed to the railing, peering at the cinder glow of Liao Xu's oncoming demon train. Up close, the sight of the flaming iron beast burned her brain. The sloping, smoke box door up front supported a ridged brow that curved back along the engine's sides. Two dirty red orbs glared down a jutting scoop of upturned, razor sharp teeth. The single light that was its nose, now muted and downturned.

It pulled along a series of passenger cars, drawing Nina's gaze. Her heart beat a shallow tattoo at seeing them filled with the undead. Moaning heads stuck out the windows. Deadun arms waved in morbid greeting, swimming in cinders thrown up from the underbelly.

"God Almighty," Pa said, his voice quavering at seeing the horde of deaduns crammed into the cars. "That's how Liao plans to do it. Transport the biters over the railway."

"I see now, my old enemy." Mathias rubbed his stubbly chin. "Splendidly vile, as usual."

"You sound excited, Father," Pa responded, a hint of fire in his voice.

Mathias shook his head. "No, Lincoln, just…" The priest sighed, weary eyes staring out at the monstrosity that rumbled toward them. "No. More struck by his tenacity, I suppose. Seems no matter what credit I give Liao, he manages to rise above even that considerable sum."

George Daggett squeezed out onto the deck then, winded from moving back and forth between the engine, the tender, and the luxury car. He stopped cold when he saw Liao Xu's hell-train. "Shit! Shit, shit, *shee-it!* But ya'll said…"

Father Mathias struck a poignant pose, as if gauging his next impossible approach. "*Fucking figures*, wouldn't you say, Mister Daggett?"

Nina barely registered the priest using George's favorite catchphrase. George himself didn't even seem to notice; he just shook his head and fetched a heavy sigh, then curled his lip and slapped his hand against the door frame. "Guess I'll go back up front and tell the boys we gotta get this sonofabitch train a'peelin.'"

CHAPTER THREE

They retreated inside the armored car so they wouldn't have to look at the damnable thing bearing down on them. Pa sat on a bunk and sighed. "I hate to shine a negative light on things, but you and Red Thunder were right. I reckon we're genuinely buggered."

The corner of her mouth lifted in a wry smile, even though her stomach twisted in fear. "Since when *ain't* we been, Pa?"

Mathias began his pacing routine, from one side of the car to the other, thinking hard, burning off the excess energy so his brain didn't pop out of his skull, Nina imagined.

Jasmine backed across the cabin, bathed in red light and shadow, her eyes darted from Father Mathias to outside.

She fell to her knees, put her hands together. "What do we do now? What now, Father?" Her voice lifted in octaves as fear consumed her. "Do we pray?"

Rachel Buell lingered near the door, her filthy dress blood red in that baleful light. "It's going to catch us."

As if in response, the train bucked. The piston *ping* and clatter took on a sudden urgency, staccato bursts of steam and the *blat* of their own whistle filling their ears.

Pa cocked his ear, his hair sticking out in wild tufts. "Sounds like the boys up front got 'er goin.'" Then he looked at the devilish train still coming hard and frowned. "Probably don't matter how hard we push now..."

"You're right, Mister Weaver. Liao's monster will shortly be upon us. Which begs the question, what next?" A long silence ensued as Father Mathias went to the threshold. He put one hand against the car's door frame, the other running through his longish hair. Bathed in that demonic glow, he appeared to be weighing options, if they had any left. Nina was feeling none too optimistic.

Suddenly, the priest said, "I had hoped it would not come to this. We couldn't derail it by destroying the track, but the creature is made of fire, some elemental spirit Liao has mustered from the depths of Perdition, no doubt." He turned and looked directly at Nina. "We must fight this hellish fire with fire of our own."

Nina wasn't sure what the Black Robe was getting at. And why the blazes he was looking only at her. "Got another fool's errand for me?"

"Our friend Red Thunder says you've touched certain... *entities.*" Mathias inclined his head at a slipshod stack of crates, and Nina saw the Indian squatting there, hardly noticeable in the shadows. The priest looked back at her, his eyes imploring.

What was he asking her for? Nina had no idea how to actively *touch* anyone—or anything, for that matter. All she had was the promise of a dream and the possibility that she'd tapped into some latent power within herself. But to channel that, to put it to good use, that was a damned different story. Hell, she'd just *now* started believing in all this magic business anyhow.

She shot the Indian a look and crossed her arms over her chest. "One step back, Father. Why a train? Why can't the spirit just fly through the air if it can get over a ruined bridge?"

"The track is merely a guide, a path for the beast. Liao found it easier to manifest his evil in the shape of one of mankind's greatest corruptions; the iron horse. The *train*. It can navigate small breaks in the path, it seems, but it cannot take flight, far as I believe."

"The train?" Pa snorted. "What's so corrupt about a train?"

Red Thunder stood. "What he says is true. The white man knows only consumption. He leaves behind ruin and calls it progress. He spreads for the sake of spreading, takes for taking, mines rock from the hills, and runs unheeding from his sins. Liao Xu will find it easier to work his magic wherever life is already poisoned, where death is in abundance. Nowhere does death abound more than *wasichu's* metal serpent."

Nina studied her father's brooding face and knew he had nothing to counter with. The same sentiment in different words had come from his own lips.

"As *wasichu* gorges on the flesh of the hills and forests," the Indian continued, "so Liao Xu is the retch of greed and gluttony."

"Hold on." Pa raised a hand. "Don't be leashing that dog to all us just because of the tone of our skin."

Nina shifted uncomfortably. "Sounds to me like you want Liao to win."

Red Thunder shook his head. " Liao Xu is the same as *wasichu's* evil, he just wears a sorrier pelt. There are a few among the white man who offer hope for peace." He glanced at Pa and gave a subtle nod. "With Liao, there is only damnation."

Pa sighed. "Well, we can philosophize all day, but what's your plan, Father?"

Mathias took out his Bible, gripped it tightly against his chest. "At first I thought I could simply bless an object, like this bundle of coal Nina brought up, then roll it off and let it burn through that evil machine." He made a fire motion with his fingers. "But I'm not so sure. The coal is of this land. We need someone connected."

"What about the key?" Pa asked.

Mathias shook his head. "I'm not confident in the key as a conduit, in this case. All the faith in the world could not be channeled through it, but perhaps there's something Liao has not counted on."

"What's that?"

"A champion of the native People." Father Mathias extended his hand, gesturing for Nina to approach him.

She looked around at the others. Pa's nod bolstered her resolve. She went to the priest, her heart pounding in her chest. In her peripheral vision, outside, the light of the demon train had grown stronger, surging to consume them.

"You've heard the drums. The voices. You have a spiritual connection to the People and the Land."

The blood rushed to Nina's face, although she couldn't say why. Was it because of her mixed heritage? Would she always feel inadequate because of that? "They're just dreams."

"Do *you* believe in them? Have you borne witness to anything *strange?*"

Nina could hardly think. The demon train barreled toward them, just a quarter mile away now, unnerving her senses with its racket. Yes, she'd easily experienced her spirit brothers and sisters, and the *boha gande*, too. Not only in the dream, but while fighting Liao in the fort, in the tunnel, and most recently on top of the tender car as she brought back the bundle of coal. A few days ago she might have brushed those incidents off, but the fact she stood here now was testament to that power. There was absolutely no reason to doubt it now.

"I reckon, but I'm no champion. I ain't no great leader." She'd wanted her voice to sound strong and brave, but it came out raspy and unsure.

A gust of heat blew through the cabin door, tossing the priest's hair around. He gave that bemused grin of his that confused and irked her. "Only one way to find out," Mathias said, then took Nina by the hand and led her out into the uncanny heat.

They stepped onto the deck, and Nina gulped, her mouth and throat dry, her *soul* parched. She shielded her eyes and gazed at the hellish, barrel-shaped engine as it glowed and stretched like a piece of anvil-sore lead, driving the stench of sulfur before it. The sound was almost unbearable; shaking, *clanking*, and *chugging* itself into a furious drone. Its upturned teeth vibrated with rail-song. Something *ping-ping-pinged* deep inside its iron shell, raw materials pushed beyond their breaking points.

It hated them, Nina knew. It hated them and would crush them to pieces, mind and body, in just another few minutes. The *Magpie* couldn't outrun it. Nina suspected nothing could. Whatever they were going to do, they needed to do it now.

She tore her gaze away from the beast and nodded to Father Mathias.

The priest stooped and untied the makeshift sack, picking out a single piece of coal. He held it up. The obsidian chunk seemed to absorb the ruddy light, but other than that, there was nothing special about it.

Nina pursed her lips, then shouted to be heard over the roar of their pursuer. "You want me to throw a durn rock at it?"

Mathias out-shouted the train's own fiery voice—and it *was* a voice, no mistake. A belching, horrible growl that chewed through every other sound. "No. I want you to bless it!"

"*What?*"

"Bless the coal, Nina, for it *is* the Land. Tree, leaf, and insect compressed over time into this one black stone."

Nina wanted to knock it out of his hand, thinking he was playing a game with her. Teasing her. "You bluffing? This is your *plan?*"

"It's a perfect conduit." Mathias held it out reverently, even as the demon train belted out an intrusive, ear-bending whoop.

"I thought you said I was the conduit? Whatever the hell that is."

The train whooped again and Nina turned to the rail, her frustration boiling over. "Shut up! Just shut the *fuck* up! Leave us alone. We never asked for this..." But she was small, her voice sucked away.

The forest caught fire at the demon train's passing. The hills and mountains were nothing but an afterthought, washed away in its wake. The hell train became *everything*.

A hand touched lightly on Nina's shoulder. "I will help you, sister. Close your eyes."

Nina looked at Red Thunder, the imposing Nez Perce suddenly standing there with them, his long black hair billowing around his stark features. She felt like she could trust in him in a way she couldn't trust anyone else, save for Pa. Nina closed her eyes and let the sulfuric heat wash across her face, let the locomotive sound storm into her ears. The rumble of the rail vibrated her aching muscles.

Red Thunder guided her hand to the rock, and all three of them held the bit of coal up. "Forget the beast. Forget Liao and the walking dead. Focus only on your dream, on your fallen Shoshone, and all the People."

Nina's lungs protested the hot, dry heat. In truth, her instincts told her to leap from the train, to throw herself from the beast's path, to get as far away as she could. But she gripped the rail even harder, determined to stand her ground. "It is...difficult. It burns. We're going to die."

"Everyone journeys to the Shadow Lands in time," Red answered. "But right now your mission is here in this world. Think of the *boha gande's* words."

Nina remembered the *boha gande* speaking to her from the inner circle, surrounded by the People's life force. *You must save the Land…a great poison runs through it, an infection that must be purged.*

"It must be purged," Nina whispered.

"That's right, Nina…" said Mathias, then the priest's voice faded away.

Nina no more. Ninataku, Fire Eater…

Fire Eater.

She swallowed nervously, squeezed her eyes shut, and breathed deep. Her lungs were not burned away. The air, while warm, was no more harmful to her than a mild zephyr on a spring day, blowing down from the high cliffs.

Drums sounded, faintly at first, gathering volume as she allowed herself to sink deeper into Shadow. The darkness filled her with the gentle calm of a placid lake in the height of summer. It seeped through her soul, through her pores, a cool mystical power intruding upon the real world—just like Liao's demon train.

Someone gasped. Nina opened her eyes and glanced over her right shoulder. Jasmine stood in the cabin doorway, her eyes fixed on the tracks, tears moistening her coffee-and-cream skin and drying almost as quickly as they ran. Rachel hid behind her, peeking over Jasmine's bare shoulder.

Pa slipped past the two females, stepped onto the deck, ignoring the behemoth on the tracks behind them. He looked Nina square in her eyes, seemed taken aback by something he saw, yet never wavered.

Pa nodded.

She looked at Father Mathias, then at the simple lump of coal held between them. The priest gripped the rail with his other hand, eyes closed, hair flying in the wind, lips moving in quiet prayer. He had faith; not only in his God, but in *her*.

From the corner of her eyes, Nina spied the encroaching beast. It flared viciously, brilliantly, spitting cinders that rained over them in ashen gray. It came on, fifty, forty, now thirty feet away.

Nina closed her eyes, hoping she could find something to say, some eloquent prayer to disarm the thing, to send it away. But she had no words, not in English nor her native tongue; she could hardly think straight, much less pray in a language she rarely spoke, but the drums beat on, their rhythm thrilling her heart to match their pace. The *boha gande* called her name. Feathers brushed against her cheeks.

Jasmine and Pa cried out. Rachel screamed from inside the armored car.

Nina's eyes flew open. The demon train reared, bloating in form, pushing a wave of searing heat over them, stirring the ash into a blizzard. Nina gazed into the undercarriage of the massive machine, tons of molten iron lifting completely off the tracks.

How in the blazes...?

Nina let go of the rail and raised her hand. She felt the intense heat against her palm, yet she didn't burn. She absorbed it. Bright tendrils of firelight coalesced from the searing belly of the beast down each of her fingers. The blistering hotness passed through her body, through the train deck, and into the land.

Fire Eater.

The name was a mantra, bounding through her skull, over and over again, demanding she accept its calling.

The demon train slammed down on the tracks. Steam poured through its whistle, its sharpened teeth gnashed. Nina didn't know if she could stop it.

But maybe...

"Keep time with me," Nina shouted. She slapped her hand against the rail, making one of the patterns she'd heard so many times in her head. The pulse of the Goshute.

Bom-bom-tata-bom, bom-bom-tata-bom...

The sound should have been swept away in the chaos, but her strikes against the rail were like a distant thunder rolling over the mountains. They cleaved the air, bullets bound for the ears of those around her.

Father Mathias gave a strange look, then followed suit, his hand awkwardly mimicking the pattern against the rail. His rhythm was questionable, but the intent was there.

Red Thunder bent low, his worn leather moccasins kicking up ash and coal dust as he danced to her rhythm, adding his voice, chanting "Yo-Hey-Ohee" over and over. In Nina's mind, Shoshone feet shuffled along with her cadence, further channeling the earth force, which fed off the chaotic energy. She saw ghost images joining Red on the deck, even the rushing air beyond filled with the chanting, dancing tribes of Shoshone, and Paiute, even Washoah, and her mother's people, the Goshute—braves, elders, women—all singing their war cries in unison.

Awash in this newfound power, Nina turned to the rail, stared down Liao's hellish beast. Her fear burned away in its heat, joining the ash that whirled about. She was hardly able to comprehend what they'd just done—what *she'd* just done.

The demon train slowed, hesitating, engine dimming,

drawing back from them like a cuffed dog. Then its iron-warped nostrils flared, lantern eyes burning with malice. It seemed about to charge again when new sounds fought through the ruckus. Clacking metal against metal. Nina looked back to see Jasmine beating a rifle barrel against the side of the deck in time with her and Father Mathias. Jasmine stood precariously close to the edge of the deck. If the monstrosity came again, it would probably knock her off, but she didn't seem to care, fixing the beast with a glare and a snarl twisting her lips. "Come on!" she yelled.

Rachel drew up on the other side of Father Mathias, a pair of empty whiskey bottles in her hands. She looked at Nina with a firm, adult expression, and *clinked* the glass bottoms against the rail, while Pa clapped a counter beat against the train car's door frame. Nina looked at her father and, in spite of Hell all around, she saw a smile spread across his face. They felt the power of the Land and its People welling about them, and through her.

Bom-bom-tata-bom, bom-bom-tata-bom...

Nina grinned back at Pa, unable to help herself. The slack, undisciplined ensemble began to tighten up, a rhythmic groove driven louder, flooding her with the same positive energy she'd felt in her dream. Nina's hips swayed, moving to the simple rhythm, giving in to it.

Bom-bom-tata-bom, bom-bom-tata-bom...

The demon train snorted, more ash than cinder now, wounded, cowed against this united front of primal *plinks* and *clanks*. Somehow, without having a damned clue, they'd hurt it!

Nina raised a brow at Father Mathias.

"The Almighty Creator is with you, sister."

Her once-questionable faith felt firmly rooted now, grounded by Red Thunder's words about converging beliefs and his faith in Father Mathias. So be it. If her native brother could believe such, she would be a fool to do otherwise. "It's time," she said.

They released the piece of coal. The black rock hovered, spinning, motes of crystal luminance flying away like water spray. Then it fell to the tracks, bouncing once before the iron beast gulped it down, moving too quick to avoid it.

The train began to choke, engine sputtering. It drew back, lantern eyes winking, as if in pain. It suddenly seemed like a normal train. The swollen sides collapsed. Its whine became a twisting iron sound, its whistle trailing off.

Sunlight broke through the clouds on the horizon as the demon train shuddered and cringed. Cool air rushed past, washing away the scent of sulfur and replacing it with the fresh smells of leaf, dirt, and hill. They pulled away from the dying locomotive as it gasped, black smoke sputtering to gray. A quarter mile. A mile. The land sped by, foothills of rough grass and scree.

Nina took a deep breath, enjoying the clean, crisp air in her lungs after the rancid heat of the beast. The spirits faded with the monstrosity, shadows drifting back to oblivion, to some distant place Nina had brushed too closely with.

She shivered. She was Nina Weaver again. Not Ninataku. Not Fire Eater. Not a warrior. Nothing but a girl with a gun now, still possessed of a living heart that thundered in her chest.

Father Mathias beamed at her, his dark eyes filled with joyous mirth. He put an arm around Rachel, brought her into the circle, and squeezed the girl. "Praise God."

Before Nina could reply, she found herself caught up in Jasmine's rough embrace. The woman gave her a half spin, laughing and whooping, her curlicue locks whipping about. "Whatever you did, it was *amazing*. It was like back home—like with my folks at worship. That feelin' you get when..." Jasmine trailed off, her smile fading slightly, as if remembering something she'd locked away with her youth and all the innocence lost along with it.

Pa clasped hands with Red Thunder, then looked at Nina with a look she'd never seen before in his eyes. She wasn't sure what it was, but it made her feel good. "We shoulda been burnt to cinders, Nina. You saved us."

"Not me." The praise made her awkward, and she hugged Jasmine again to release the nervous tension. "It was all of us. Father Mathias's blessing. Red Thunder's war dance. Your horrible racket." She smiled at her father. "I'd been lost without all of you."

Pa chuckled. The moment was genuine and her heart swelled. It was the first time she felt something like real hope blossom deep inside since...well, since a long, long time ago.

Rachel stood nearby, arms crossed. Jasmine put her arm out and said, "Come here, girl," and Rachel stepped in, hugging Jasmine and Nina both. Nina embraced the teenager firmly, feeling a sense of kinship, and then a shadow from inside the armored car caught her attention.

James Manning filled the doorway, resting a hand on Pa's shoulder. He was covered in coal dust, sweating as she figured he would be. A sight for sore eyes.

Looks like they'd have a little more time together after all.

But then she noticed others moving around inside the car, as well. Strobridge's face peeked over Manning's shoulder. His voice was strained. "You got rid of the devil's engine."

"We—" Mathias started to say before Strobridge cut him off.

"Ain't got time for another one of your stories, Thomas, much as I know you love tellin' 'em. Y'all best get inside." The railroad boss disappeared without another word.

Pa looked into the car, then at Manning, his smile gone. "If all of you are back here, who's running the train?"

"That's just it," Manning said, his voice hoarse. "We're coming down the mountain too fast and there's some mighty steep curves ahead. The boiler's leaking steam and there's nothing can be done about it. The brakes just aren't getting the pressure we need."

"So what does that mean?" Jasmine asked.

Manning looked at her, then his gaze cut to Nina and stayed. "It means best we all get inside, batten down, and hold on for our lives. Maggie's going off the rails."

CHAPTER FOUR

WHEN NINA THOUGHT OF James Manning back in bed with his arms around her, this wasn't what she had in mind. It had been her pa's idea, using the cotton-stuffed mattresses from the bunks for padding. Now he was on one side of her and Manning on the other, all of 'em hunkered down with their hands and feet locked into the rungs of the turret ladder and the bedding pulled around their shoulders. Jasmine and Father Mathias were across from them, Rachel tucked between them.

Morning light seeped in through the gun holes and turret frame, and the *Magpie* shuddered and whined while her engine panted like a mad dog. The gritty scent of coal

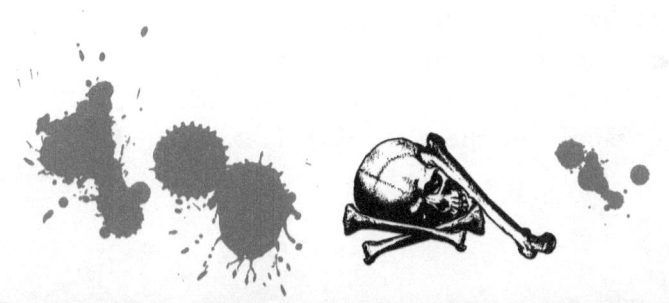

dust and unwashed bodies pressed too close assaulted Nina's nostrils. She looked at Pa and he gave her hand a squeeze and held it there. After everything they'd endured, she wouldn't have thought they'd be done for in the belly of a runaway train. Wasn't how she pictured the end, but come think of it, she hadn't pictured it being served up as deadun chow neither.

Jasmine's voice drew her attention. "You okay?"

Rachel answered. "Aside from y'all crushing me."

"Just gonna keep crushin' you till this is all over, if you don't mind," Jasmine said, her eyes reflecting fear back at Nina.

Rachel sniffed, worming her hand up to rub her soot-coated nose. "What's the point? We're about to meet my folks. Might as well pray and hope it comes quick." Rachel's tone was an eerie reminder of Clara Buell and, once more, Nina's heart ached for the girl with tragical affinity.

"Let's all pr—" Mathias started to say when the car abruptly jumped beneath them, lifting Nina's rump off the floor and depositing it back down. Ammunition boxes shifted, straining against the ropes Red Thunder had used to secure them. She couldn't see the Indian, though.

"Goddammit," George Daggett said from behind them.

Nina locked her foot around one of the rungs to keep from sliding. To her right Pa had his forehead pressed against the steel turret. His hand squeezed hers hard, then Manning, on her other side, wriggled his arm beneath hers and hitched them tight to one another.

The car settled for a second, then hopped again even harder this time before they had a chance to catch their breaths. It leaned, and the groan of iron reverberated through the car. The floor quaked beneath them and Rachel screamed as the small cannon in the turret rattled. Loose shells rained down over them with metallic *pings*. Then the angle increased and they slid toward the wall.

Nina cussed as she tried to keep her foot locked. Manning reached out to grab a closer rung.

"Hold on!" Pa hollered.

Rachel and Jasmine were both screaming, and another voice yelled, "Here we go!"

Nina swore she heard Buck Patterson yell *yee-haw* just before a sharp *snap* cut through the steel-wheel drone. The car lurched and slammed back down. The connection to the luxury car must've broke, likely sending it tumbling off the rails.

But what about the tender car and engine? Crashing sounds reached her ears, the screech of iron and steel, a series of loud thumps, an explosion, then a liver-ripping impact. Every joint in Nina's body tried to separate, and her head struck the ladder rung. Cinders and debris blasted through the turret frame. The front of their car bounced, jumped, tilted over.

And then they were airborne, Pa's hand torn away from her grasp, Manning gone, too. Nina's stomach lurched with the sudden weightlessness as the side of the car became the roof. She wanted to scream but nothing escaped her lungs, her breath just wouldn't come. Something smacked her back, her head, her legs, then she went numb. She plunged feet over shoulders as the opposite side of the car jumped up to meet her. Someone slammed into her, and it was peculiar that her first thought was she hoped it was her pa and maybe she'd broken his fall a little bit. A grunt tore from her as she rolled head over heels…

Various moans came first. Nina opened her eyes. She must have blacked out. She came to among a mess of crushed crates and other scraps of unidentifiable wreckage. She didn't dare move for a couple minutes. When she did, it was to check her foot, then the other, now a leg and hand, making sure everything worked. She pushed herself to her knees and looked around, her brain still bouncing inside her battered skull.

Everything was slantwise. She saw Strobridge tangled in some pull-down bed frames on the side of the car—which was now the floor—working himself loose, coughing and cursing. She blinked, trying to clear her head as she looked for Pa and James, instead saw Father Mathias and Red Thunder near the mid-section, the Indian helping the priest to his feet. She started seeing two of each of 'em so she blinked again, then sighted Rachel hanging from the crosswise turret ladder, her hair hanging inches from the floor. Nina prayed she wasn't dead, but the girl didn't look to be moving. She kept scanning the car but couldn't make out anyone else.

"Nina. Nina…" A moaning voice, nearby.

"Pa?"

She searched around in the dusty light creeping in through the turret hole. She knee-walked through the clutter and found her father beneath a smashed box of rifles. "Pa! I'm here." She pulled the bottom part of the crate, and the entire cluster of well-oiled rifles clacked as they spilled free.

"Nina." He smiled, his face a bloody mess. "You all right?"

"Don't move," she said, checking him for open wounds

and broken bones, wincing at the weakness in her limbs and her shifting vision.

Manning crawled out of the darkness from behind more debris. He struggled to his feet and moved his right arm around, grimacing, then rubbed at his jaw.

"You all right?" she asked, her mouth dry.

He nodded, or at least she thought he did. She was too dazed to know for certain.

She starting clearing more rifles off her pa and Manning stumbled over. They helped him sit up, and more blood coursed down the side of his face. He rubbed at it with his sleeve, smearing a dark stain across his cheek and into his beard.

"You got a bleeder on your scalp, Pa."

"I figured that."

"How's your foot?"

"I think the rest of me's caught up with it." He cleared his throat and began looking around. "How is everybody?" he called out.

Nobody answered right away, except for Strobridge, who was doing his damndest to hack up his lungs. She rather hoped he'd broke a few ribs—or better yet, his pecker.

"Sound off, everyone," Pa said in a gruff tone.

"Let's just get you outside, Lincoln," Manning said. "Then we can take a head count."

Nina nodded, but then heard Jasmine yell, "Rachel!"

She looked over to see Jasmine, her lower half shrouded in darkness, pulling at Rachel's limp body. "Help me," she said, and Red Thunder hurried over, grabbed the girl, and freed her body from the ladder.

"Is she alive?" Jasmine asked.

"Let's get her out and have a look," Father Mathias said, motioning for them to follow. "Let's go, everyone." He climbed over the ladder and through the open turret hole, turning and extending his arms for the Indian to hand Rachel over.

Nina took a quick assessment of the train car. The top part of the frame had been ripped completely free, leaving plenty of room to crawl through. That's when she saw Buck, hanging from the ceiling by one leg. She pointed him out and Manning went over.

"He's alive," James said.

Then Mason Daggett popped up from nowhere, dripping wet and reeking like a still. "Where's George?"

Manning turned, about to speak, when a weak voice floated up. "I think…you're standing on me…" it said.

Mason and James looked down and started clearing debris. They extracted George from beneath the mess, covered in blood, oil, and feathers from a split mattress. They checked him over, then worked at getting Buck down, who came to during the process ready to fight. He took a few swings, still hanging upside-down, while Manning yelled, "Buck! It's us!" and Mason hollered, "Calm the hell down!" He did, but not before belting the dazed George in the side of his noggin and making the man's knees buckle.

"Christ!" George yelled after he regained his footing. He glared at Buck as Manning and Mason finally wedged him out.

Buck was wild-eyed, his shock of hair sticking out every which way, and he glared at them for a moment, breathing heavily. Manning put a hand on the roughrider's shoulder, saying, "You all right, Buck?"

The man gave a glassy stare, then grunted and nodded.

"That's everyone," Pa said, leaning on Nina and wiping more blood from his forehead and away from his eyes. "Come on. Let's just get out of here and take stock."

They had to help Buck, George, and her pa through the hole, laying an intact mattress over the jagged metal. Once they were outside, Nina took a look around. The engine and tender car had flipped on the track, which accounted for the impact that derailed the armored car. The engine lay inside the curve, tilted in a bed of soft sand, leaking plumes of dark steam and tongues of flame from a crack along its side. The tender car lay nearby, *outside* the curve, also flipped over, coal and water spilling out onto the ground.

The luxury car with all their supplies had been thrown completely clear, rolling several times, it seemed, before smashing through thickets of *chaparro* and a bunch of now-broken Joshua trees. The front deck was mired in a shallow creek that ran beneath a trestle bridge.

She looked back at the gun car. After colliding with the engine and jumping the tracks, they had dropped fifteen or twenty feet before the car cut a furrow through a bank of soft dirt and skidded to a halt. *Lucky*. Maybe the one damn lucky thing so far…aside from everyone being alive, of course.

She peered to where Father Mathias and Jasmine had Rachel awake and sitting up. Nina breathed easier. She hadn't expected any of them to survive. Now it looked as if they all had.

Thank you, boha gande.

The thought that surprised her even more was that she *was* thankful for everyone being alive. The day before they were at one another's throats, letting lead fly, ready to do murder. She had wanted to end Strobridge more than once, but at the moment she was just thankful and that was that. Plenty of time to hate the sonofabitch later.

Something howled *WOOO*, causing her to start and her hand to go to her holster. The demon train came out between stands of tall pines along the track. It puttered down the rise, hauling its cargo of deaduns. Nina bared her teeth. There went all her happy thoughts, scattered like dry leaves in a bleak wind.

Liao's diseased minions were spreading across the land, and seeing them chugging along amidst the wreckage of the *Magpie* rekindled her anger. Nina's face hardened, as did everyone's, and they all paused to watch the devil and his servants go by. Jasmine had her hand on Rachel's shoulder, her other hand to her chest. Mason launched some spit. George watched in a daze, blinking. Nina looked at Father Mathias, who stood hands-on-hips, observing Liao's train cross the bridge and chug out of sight.

"Well," Manning said from next to her, "I suppose that is that."

"That is *what?*"

He shrugged.

"Where you reckon he's taking them, Jaz?" Rachel asked.

Jasmine shook her head. "Lord knows."

No one knew the answer. They could only speculate.

"Away is all I give a good goddamn about," Strobridge said, then cleared his throat and started making small coughing noises again. He covered his beard with his sleeve.

Nina ran a hand through her ragged hair. "We can't worry ourselves over it now. We got other things to take care of."

"She's right," Manning said. "Let's get whatever supplies together we can. Look for anything we can use to clean and dress wounds, then food and blankets or whatever we can find to keep warm come night." He set off for the gun car.

"Hold on," Strobridge walked toward Manning and fell in step with him, jawing and hawking phlegm as they walked. Whatever he was spitting out seemed a might dark to Nina's eyes.

Mason started tearing strips of cloth for bandages. "We could use some water. Whiskey, too," he called after Manning and Strobridge, then went to one knee beside his brother. George's face was covered in blood, much like Pa's, but where her father was making sense, the Daggett mumbled mostly nonsense—*more so than usual*—plus she figured Buck's fist probably hadn't helped matters none.

"Red Thunder and I will go down to the supply car," Father Mathias announced. "If there's anything left unbroken, we'll bring it up."

"I'll help," Jasmine said.

Rachel included herself. "Me, too."

Jasmine peered at her. "You should stay here and rest. You was out cold."

"I'm okay." The girl stood, then raised her brows. "See?" She seemed steady enough, and her face was determined, daring them to tell her different.

Nina could see Jasmine wanted to argue, but the fact was no matter how sorry or protective she was feeling for the white girl, no black woman—especially a woman of her ilk, free or not—told a white woman what to do; in spite of Rachel's thirteen or some odd years, her days of child's play were done and gone.

"All right," Jasmine inclined her head. "Whatever you think's best."

"Shave tail's getting some sass," Mason said without looking over.

"What now?" Nina said, curling her lip. "You taking over blather-mouthin' obligations since George cracked his nut?"

"Just making an observation."

"Well, no one asked you."

Mathias, Jasmine, Rachel, and Red Thunder hadn't heard them evidently and made their way down the small hill toward the creek and the supply car.

"Let it be, Nina," Pa said. "Not going to do any of us any good to get our dander up over mere words."

"Better listen to your pa," Mason said, then gave a contemptuous snort.

Nina chewed the inside of her lip, then knelt next to her father. Buck was sitting nearby on the grassy, rock-strewn incline, just leaning back on a flat rock and feeling the sun on his face.

"He's just sounding off because he's worried like the rest of us," Pa said low so Mason didn't hear. "Don't play into it. You're smarter than that."

Nina nodded, then peered at Buck's wounded leg. "How is it?"

The roughrider looked at her and his skin had a sickly pallor to it. He seemed a bit shaky, too. Even so, he shrugged. "I'm fine. Just aggravated it a bit, that's all."

It looked like more than just aggravation to Nina, though—the man's buckskins were bloody, and the stains looked mighty fresh. "You had it looked at since last night?"

Buck huffed beneath his mustache. "You're seein' the injury plain." But when Nina's eyes wouldn't let him loose, his hard bravado melted. "If you're askin' whether someone looked at it in a doctorly way, that'd be no."

"Take 'em off then."

He narrowed his eyes, sucked at his teeth a bit, and Nina knew he wished he had a right plug of *baccy* in there.

"You need to get them trousers off, Mister. Someone needs to take a look at that wound. If it gets infected..."

"She's right, Buck," Pa said. "You let that go and you'll lose a lot more than your pride."

"I ain't a *goldurned* child. You think I don't know about infection? I had three arrowheads burned out of my back in '59, lost this finger in '63 to a meanspirited sidewinder." He held up a three-fingered left hand, which was the first time she'd noticed it. "I've had my fair share of festerment and venom, trust me."

"Then you know why we should get you fixed up." Nina stared at the man until Pa gave him a reassuring half-smile.

The roughrider groused and eyeballed her father. "What about that," he said, motioning to Pa's head wound.

"I'm seeing to it, too." Nina's gaze didn't waver.

"She always like this?"

"Surly as the day is long," Pa said.

Nina crossed her arms.

"Take 'em off right here? Don't seem right."

Manning walked up with a crate of supplies in hand. "What don't seem right?"

"Your lady friend here wants me to drop my drawers."

Manning looked at Nina, at Buck, then Pa, and seemed amused with Buck's timidity. "Afraid of showin' off Lil'

Buck, are you?"

Nina chuckled at that as she took a blanket out of Manning's crate, then stifled her amusement upon seeing Buck's scowl.

The roughrider sighed and dropped the dark expression. "Look. It's just…ain't a soul seen my pecker since my dear departed Mary went on through the Pearly Gates ahead o' me."

They were quiet a second, then Pa patted Buck's shoulder and nodded knowingly. "I'll check him, Nina." He looked up at James. "Any bandages or the like?"

Manning tossed him a bundle of torn cloth as Red Thunder and Mathias returned already, carrying a clay jug and an armful of whiskey bottles, respectively. "A lot to salvage amongst the mess down there; certainly enough to get us through a few nights," the priest declared. He looked around. "Where is Mister Strobridge?"

"Still in the gun car," Manning answered.

Nina put the blanket around Pa's shoulders as he unrolled the bundle of bandages, mostly bedsheets torn into strips, though she recognized a few bits of ribbons from Jasmine's torn skirt, too.

"Padre," Mason called over from where he knelt next to George. He waved for one of the bottles.

"Of course." Father Mathias lowered the bundle of clinking glass, took an amber bottle and walked it over.

"No."

"What do you mean?"

Mason pointed to the label. "That's Kentucky bourbon. That ain't for wounds. Give me some of that white-eye in the clear bottle there. Nasty Injun whiskey. Although…"

He snatched the bourbon from the priest. "You can leave this here with me and Georgie."

Mason twisted the top off and tossed some back while Mathias fetched the maize whiskey and handed it over. Mason set the bourbon down and poured a splash of the cheap stuff on a folded rag. He wiped the blood off George's forehead, mopping his hair to the side, and found the source of the wound, a nasty gash running from his crown to top of his forehead.

Some of the liquor ran down George's face and neck, and he sputtered. Mason shoved the tip of the bottle in his brother's mouth and turned it up. Any normal man would have choked, but George took to it like a suckling lamb. Mason pulled the bottle away after five or six swigs, and George let some dribble from his bloody mouth and murmured himself back into a stupor.

Nina sighed at the whole display, then did the same for Pa, flushing his scalp with spirits and dabbing it as clean as she could. His wound didn't seem near as bad as George's, so she was glad for that. Once she'd cleaned him up, she said she was going to go help the girls "rustle through some stuff."

"Careful," Pa told her, working out some kinks in his neck.

Nina gave a half wave and started off toward the tilted luxury car. "Be over-careful!" he hollered, and she waved again.

The sun was painting the sky a baby blue as it rose, poking in and out amidst a canvas of long clouds fleeing east. The most towering crags of the Sierra Nevada range were behind them, and a steady breeze skirled down, causing the sage brush to shimmy on the rocky slopes. Nina reckoned the first thing she'd look for is something warm to replace—or at least cover—the crusty, torn plaid shirt she had on.

She descended toward the babbling creek, stepped over some snapped trees, and twisted rods of metal, as well as other scattered debris. The train car's wheels had been torn off, the side panels ripped free, and the roof crunched in. It was plumb luck they hadn't been caught in that beat up tin can.

She could hear the women inside as she climbed up on the deck and went in. Jasmine and Rachel were rummaging through piles of stuff. The contents of the entire car were shook nearly to pieces. Jasmine stuffed something beneath her girdle, glancing at Nina.

"What do you have there, squirrelly girl?"

Jasmine sighed and pulled out a folded stack of bills. "Must have got shaken loose in the crash."

Nina laughed. "Figures that bastard has money tucked away all over the place. I don't give a shit. Take it."

Jasmine smiled and re-stuffed the money under a breast, then went back to business.

They'd been organizing things, stacking canned goods and bundles of dried meats. Almost all of that was still in one piece, more or less. Stores of water and whiskey had been significantly reduced, but a few bottles had survived the crash. Nina opened one of the bottles of Kentucky whiskey and took a long draw before passing it to Jasmine. The black woman nodded and took a gulp, wiped her arm across her lips, and handed it back.

"That is top shelf right there," she said.

Rachel came over. "I'd like some, if you don't mind."

Nina looked at her, tucked a few strands of Rachel's light brown hair behind her small ear and cupped her chin. "You think your ma—"

Rachel pulled away, her expression clearly offended by Nina's coddling. "Ma said there was nothing wrong with it on occasion."

Nina still felt reluctant, so Rachel added, "I stole nips from Pappy's stock all the time."

"She's been through Hell." Jasmine gave a weak smile.

Nina started to hand over the bottle, then pulled it back before Rachel took it from her. "Just one swallow, you hear?"

"Just one." Rachel took the bottle, put it to her lips, and tilted it back. Twin rivers of liquor ran from the corners of her mouth and flowed down her chin. She took more than one swallow, grimacing when the burn hit her throat and belly. The girl went well past the agreed-to limit, but Nina hadn't the heart to take the bottle away from her. Rachel *had* been through Hell. Nina was more than acquainted, and the girl deserved a good whiskey numbing as much as anyone.

She finally handed the bottle back, smacked her lips, and exhaled an alcohol-scented, "*Whooo!*"

"You put a dent in it. Feel better?"

Rachel nodded and went back to rummaging.

Nina chuckled. "You probably won't later."

"Us ladies gotta stick together," Jasmine said, pulling back a cover to reveal a mound of odds and ends. She picked up two undamaged lanterns and set them aside. "Like we *always* done. That's what my ma told *me*."

"I'd agree with that, in general principle."

"General principle? Girl, let me tell you something. Men are lying, thieving bastards. Each and every one of them."

"Not my pa."

"Oh, and not Mister Manning, either, right?" Jasmine sat back on her heels, arms thrown over her knees. "Let me tell you another little something, Nina*taku*, Fire Eater. When you lain with as many men as me, you get to know their itty bitty secrets. After a good tumble they feel like children all over again. Feelin' all free to discuss all manner of indiscretions and how they feel rightfully justified doing whatever they is doin'. Confessin' their *sins*, so to speak." Jasmine shook her head and blew a shock of fluffy hair out of her face. "I respect the good priest, he's a good man of God, but I reckon I heard more than your average preacher in a year's worth of Sundays. All men got somethin' deep and dark. Trust me on that account, sweetheart."

Nina put her mouth to the side, dubious.

"And your Mister James Manning. Them good lookin' ones, they got the most secrets of all."

Nina exchanged glares with Jasmine, eyes locked, lips turned to snarls, until they could take it no longer. They burst out laughing. Rachel looked at them like they had both lost their minds.

"Let's just agree on watchin' out for one another." Nina raised the bottle in a toast.

"Amen," said Jasmine.

"Amen," Rachel echoed. "Now how about another sip?"

CHAPTER FIVE

SEVERAL SPENCER RIFLES AND some standard-issue muskets were lined up against a broken bench seat. Red Thunder, who'd been checking through salvaged ammunition pouches and spreading 'em out on the seat top, gazed up as Nina and her companions came back up the hill. She weren't half as glum, to be honest, after ladies' talk and liquor. Plus she'd managed to scrounge up a couple hanks of dried meat, some canned vittles, and a few woolen blankets, which she carried in hempen bags slung over both her shoulders.

She nodded to Red. The Indian returned the gesture, then went back to arranging bullets, obviously wanting no

part of whatever the white men were animatedly discussing a few strides off in the direction of the gun car. She looked back, making sure Jasmine and Rachel followed behind. They were ladened with traveling bags filled with canteens, more canned food, some cups and utensils, and other odd bits.

She gazed ahead again and got the feeling she'd missed part of an important conversation. The men looked as if they were arguing. Nina stepped up and laid her sacks on the ground. "What now?" she asked, directing her question at James.

He tried to keep his voice controlled, but it had a hard edge. "I'm thinking that train of deaduns is bound for Reno. As such, I propose we should skip it and head elsewhere."

Father Mathias held up a finger, shook his head politely. "And I disagree on that count."

Nina looked at the priest and railroad boss as they stood paces apart, the strain and tension growing. Strobridge grunted and worked his jaw around while glaring at Mathias. "And as I said I've got people in Carson City."

"I'm sure you do," the priest replied. "But the Taiping Jing is in Reno, right where *you* left it. And that's where we'll need to be going—Red Thunder, Buck, and myself, if no one else."

Pa was standing nearby, arms crossed, wearily shaking his bandaged head. "Surely you don't expect us to go to Reno if Liao Xu's train bore those deaduns into town?"

Mathias looked to the southern horizon. "It's God's will."

"God's will? God's will! *Pshaw!*" Strobridge gave a sort of scraunchy snort. "Look! My people will protect us in Carson City." He flung his hand at Manning. "I agree with

Manning here. There ain't no sense in going after what's already lost."

"Don't put words into my mouth, Strobridge. I didn't say anything about Carson City. I'm just suggesting we avoid Reno for obvious reasons. As to our destination, I make no insinuations."

Strobridge propped his boot up on a piece of wreckage and waved his hand. "I don't give a shit what you insinuate, as long as it ain't Reno."

"Need to get my brother to a doctor afore we do anything else." Mason Daggett stated as he sat by his brother. His Kentucky bourbon was already down to the dregs and he stopped from sopping the sweat from George's brow. Mason's eyes looked dangerous. "Fuck anyone who's got issue with that."

"Let's think about this." Pa made settling motions with his hands. "I can't agree to take my daughter into Reno until the true impact of that train chock-full of deaduns is known. Maybe we can find a place agreeable to everyone. Reno and Carson aren't the only watering holes around here."

Nina didn't speak up, but she knew her pa was wrong. She didn't understand why, but she was linked to Father Mathias and Red Thunder in their quest to stop Liao Xu. Pa might not see it, but the need to follow the Black Robe and the Nez Perce warrior sang in her veins. She would get Pa to understand, but needed to pick the right moment to talk to him.

And she hoped beyond all hope that Manning would come with them. A few days ago she'd been more concerned with getting to safety, but between then and now—

especially after this morning—she'd learned more about herself than she had in her entire life. She was bound to the People in spirit, and to her *boha gande*. What other things might she discover about herself if she continued on this path?

"What say we just stay here a spell?" Buck asked from where he laid on the embankment. "Someone's bound to see our smoke signal." He tossed his thumb at the wreck of the *Magpie* and the dark smoke that plumed from the destroyed engine's boiler.

"Salvage team was in Truckee," said Strobridge. "Ain't a soul coming. They're probably too occupied with looking for lunch, if you get me. All that smoke is doing is likely attracting more goddamn deaduns."

Nina's stomach dropped at the thought. She and the girls had been acting foolish without paying attention to their surrounds. The tall dry grass and scrub brush suddenly looked a fair bit more ominous. She took note that the same thought crossed Jasmine's mind, the woman's gaze suddenly combing the outskirts.

"So what are you suggesting we do, Lincoln?" Manning cut in.

"Well…I ain't as acquainted with the land south of Crystal Peak, but I do know we follow the river east for a spell, then due south along the edge of the foothills. Might take a couple days, but we should find a burg called Galena or somesuch. I'm thinking the hills will provide adequate cover, and we do this maybe it'll give things in Reno time to hash out. Might be the officials there will get things under control, and that'll give you," he inclined his head to Mathias, "a safe way to get your talisman." He turned his head to Strobridge. "And you can mosey on to Carson City once we reach Galena. Till then, I think best we keep one another's hindquarters safe and stay on the lookout."

Nina was surprised no one spoke out right away considering everyone's mutual dislike for everyone else, then Mason Daggett spoke up, "Ain't nothin' we can do anyways. Not with my brother and the injured." He sloshed his bottle in Buck's direction. "Ain't got the strength to pig-a-back ya'll limpers."

"Nobody's *carrying* Buck Patterson," said Buck, sour-faced.

Nina was tempted to tell Mason they could just leave George behind, just like the Daggetts wanted to do to her pa early on, but she remembered her father's words and kept her mouth clamped. No sense in stirring up more shit.

Red Thunder, quiet since the wreck, suddenly stood among them. For someone with *thunder* in their name he sure was one durned stealthy mover. "Father Mathias can help," the Indian said.

The priest looked at him. "I think it wou—"

"There are some among the Black Robes who know the secrets of miracle healing," Red Thunder continued. "The ones with enough *faith*."

"Faith? What's that?" Strobridge laughed as he placed his hands on his hips. "You never told me you was a blessed healer. Why, you're just brimmin' with secrets, Thomas."

Red Thunder bowed his dark head. "I'm sorry, Father, but you can help these people regardless what it might cost. Otherwise, we are stuck in this place, and Liao Xu's poison will spread."

Father Mathias gazed eastward along the tracks, hand

rubbing at his chin. "Might not be necessary. The Truckee River runs along the tracks, no? I believe their paths cross at certain points. Perhaps we could put together a flotation device of some kind, load up our supplies, and simply float into Reno. Town that cosmopolitan's bound to have a doctor or two."

"*If* we were going to Reno, that would be an option," Pa said. "But none of us are keen on precipitating headlong into a thousand more deaduns, Father."

"Yes. It seems the Reno option is lacking sufficient backing."

Nina decided she wanted to hear more about whatever the Sam Hill their Indian friend was talking about. "This true? You heal folks?"

Father Mathias looked tentative, then sighed. "For it became *Him*, for whom are all things—"

Strobridge hawked phlegm to the side and said, "Here we go again."

Mathias continued nonplussed, "…and by whom *are* all things, in bringing many sons unto glory, to make the captain of their salvation perfect through sufferings." The priest paused, allowing his words to sink in. "That's from the Book of Hebrews, my good people. It describes Jesus's suffering for our salvation. And God means for us to understand this suffering…"

"Even if it means suffering ourselves?" Nina asked.

"Precisely so. If I went around healing everyone, then everyone would be—"

"They'd all be healed!" Strobridge interrupted, seeming to enjoy putting Father Mathias over the philosophical barrel. "Why, we'd be out of this fix and already cuttin' a path east without anymore goddamn dickering about." The railroad boss shook his head. "Here's the honest truth. He's a pretender. He likes to put the screws to folks, pull the wool over everyone's eyes, don't you, Thomas? See, I'm a man who speaks plain. I don't climb up on a pulpit and sell lies wrapped in missionary trappings and saintly paraphernalia. The good father here doesn't have the power in him to heal *anyone!* He's a charlatan. A sanctimonious, ostentatious—yeah, see, I know them big words too, Thomas—ostentatious, malingering sham!"

Manning put a hand on Strobridge's shoulder, but the boss man didn't miss a beat. He pointed at the priest. "And Christianity is just one heaping, steaming crock of bullshit, pardon my lassitude. Bull. Shit." By the end, Strobridge had worked himself up so much he batted Manning's hand away and wiped a string of dark spittle from his scraggly salt-and-pepper whiskers.

Nina looked at the wild-eyed boss with her brows lowered and a sick feeling in her gut. Strobridge glared back, then took off his hat and stepped away. He bent and coughed a few times, his hand going to his sternum. He hawked another thick bit of sputum and straightened.

Father Mathias shook his head. "That isn't how it works," he said to Strobridge. "Make your blasphemies. Regard me with contempt. It doesn't diminish the Lord's word or his will. Not at all. Not even for one-thousandth of a malignant blow for air in those befouled lungs."

They all stood quiet until the railroad boss huffed, stalked over to the liquor crate, and snatched up a bottle. Nina was none too sure if he was gonna drink it or throw it at the priest. The man opted the former.

Pa went forward in subdued tones. "If it's God's will we all suffer while a plague of deaduns runs rampant across His green earth, so be it. I've managed to make it this far. Can't be so sure about everyone else, though."

Father Mathias smiled at Pa, his eyes taking on genuine warmth. He covered his mouth with his hand as if stifling a chuckle and shook his head. The priest sighed. "Perhaps now *is* that sparing moment when I address our burdens, if only to ultimately serve Him. Lincoln, I apologize. Everyone!" Mathias did chuckle then, and he put his hand on Red Thunder's shoulder. "Sometimes I'm blinded by my vows, my friend. You are right," he said, then addressed them all. "My willingness to suffer while lifting the Lord high in my heart sometimes causes me to be blind to the subtle messages he sends, and how brilliantly he does so. Let the words of my mouth and the thoughts of my heart be pleasing in your eyes, O Lord, my strength and my salvation. Thank you, Red Thunder, and thank you, Lincoln. I *will* heal us, God willing."

"Praise the Lord," Pa added with a huff.

Jasmine held up her hands and shook them. "Thank you, Jesus."

Nina shouldn't have been surprised at Jasmine's devotion to the white man's God. She'd seen conviction in the woman's eyes before, and her singing had evoked powerful images of divine things. It was a conviction she herself was beginning to understand.

"You religious freaks make me sick." Strobridge walked off with his open bottle. The group ignored him.

"There is one catch," Father Mathias said, his finger raised to the sky. "In order to receive the Lord's healing touch, one must have faith. You have to believe to receive." He chuckled, clearly pleased with his ability to rhyme. "I don't doubt your faith, Lincoln, but George..."

Mason Daggett's eyes narrowed, his body going stiff. "Just do what you're gonna do, Padre."

"Very well. Stand back and pray the Lord finds something redeemable within your brother."

"Don't you hurt him. Otherwise, you'll be eatin' out of your backside for the rest of your life."

Mathias bent over George. "Sounds like an unpleasant experience, Mister Daggett. Not to worry."

Mason had positioned his brother on a folded coverlet, softening up his position some. George's head and neck was damp with whiskey and a slow trickle of red ran from his ear. In Nina's approximation, he seemed to be giving his best presentation of a door nail—all limp, skin pale and lifeless, with his arms hanging at his sides. Scant movements beneath his closed lids and the gentle rise of his chest were the only indications he weren't dead just yet.

Father Mathias pulled a simple black stole and a small vial of clear liquid—which Nina assumed to be holy water—from an inner pocket. The stole had a single golden cross stitched into each end. He sprinkled it with a few drops of water and placed it directly on George's head so that the ends hung over his ears.

George sighed, his head turning up as if to greet the priest's touch.

Father Mathias spread his hand on George's crown, pulled his Bible out and began fingering through the marked sections. "Ah," he said, finding his place. He cleared his throat, and then began: "And Jesus went about all Galilee, teaching in their synagogues, and preaching the gospel of the Kingdom, and healing all manner of sickness and all manner of disease among the people."

George Daggett murmured in an oddly peaceable way.

"That's right, George. That's what Our Lord and Savior did. For even *He* understood there was a time for healing. And it took these fine folks here to make me realize it was *my* time, too. That's why I got my hand on your head, trying to infuse some of the Christ's healing into you."

"Unh," George replied. He whistled lightly between his teeth, turning his head to the left where a thin line of drool spilled down his chin.

Father Mathias dug into his Bible again. "And the people, when they knew it, followed him; and he received them, and spake unto them of the Kingdom of God, and healed them that had need of healing."

George's chest surged, as if a sudden jolt had gone through him. His mouth popped open, "Ahhh," he groaned before he settled back, murmuring to someone named Cap, and then telling his Ma it was Mason's turn to feed the pigs.

Father Mathias pressed hard on the stole, squinting his eyes shut and pursing his lips. "George Daggett, if you have any faith in God, let it be known now, as that wound of yours is naught compared to the deep pain inside of you. By Christ's wounds then, I implore you, O Lord, let this man be healed!"

George jerked awake, his eyes spinning in their sockets for a moment then focused on Father Mathias. "Who fucked me in the ear?" he asked, before falling unconscious again. Only this time, color rushed to George Daggett's skin. His breathing steadied, and his eyes calmed beneath his lids.

Father Mathias removed the stole to reveal the head wound was gone, the blood already dried up. It fell away in dark flakes.

"That's…why, that's *amazing*, Father," Pa said, his voice filled with wonder.

The rest of them ranged from speechless to dubious. Nina felt more curious than anything else. In the past three days she had witnessed all kinds of amazing things: a heavy dose of deaduns; witnessing the Black Robe's miracles and yellow-hooded Liao Xu's terrible magic back at the fort and again on the train; and especially discovering the strange powers within herself. All of the above affirmed her need to follow Mathias wherever he may roam.

Mason Daggett, rather than be grateful, scowled and stood face to face with the priest. "You question my brother's faith, you question mine. Guess we're just a couple of dirt-worshipin' heathens to you, Padre…" He emphasized the *P* with a spray of spittle. "Like your pet Injun there."

Father Mathias didn't meet Mason's glare.

"Now get the fuck away." Mason gave the priest a hard shove in the chest, making him stumble to keep his balance.

Red Thunder pulled his tomahawk free, but Father Mathias stopped him with a casual wave. "It's all right. Having one's faith questioned can stir up emotions, no doubt." He smiled weakly. "Let's see to Mister Patterson."

"You're a bully!" Rachel suddenly shouted, and Jasmine grabbed her arm to keep her from approaching Mason. "You're a brute!"

"Shut up, little girl." Mason said dismissively, bending to check his sleeping brother. "Know your place, like that wag-tail coon who thinks she's your adop—"

Nina saw red. She didn't know what she was doing until she was on top of Mason, pummeling down with closed fists. She struck him at least three good ones before someone pulled her off the mouthy bastard. Mason sprung up, stumbled, fell down, then got back up. He started forward.

"Don't," Manning said, not to Nina but to Mason. He had a tight grip on both her arms, but let go of one and placed himself between them. "You're sauced and you've got too much Rebel soldier in you, Mason. That's what? Your third bottle?"

"Rein in that bitch squaw of yourn…or I swear…"

"You won't do a blamed thing, son," her Pa said. "Go see to your brother and when you dry up everyone can make nice again."

Mason panted, his face covered in coal dirt, bruises, scrapes, and spit. His gaze roved over them, and she reckoned he was weighing the situation in his own roostered estimation, seeing it was pretty much him against everyone else.

Strobridge came striding out from behind some scrub, adjusting his trousers. "I'd do as he says, Mason. No sense stirring more shit up than we need." Nina wondered if Strobridge was parodying Pa or being serious.

"Listen to you," Mason groused. "Got no place to fuckin' talk."

"The difference is I'm sober and still spewed my ungenerous shit. Learn a lesson from your elders, especially when they go off half-cocked like a deuced-up fool."

"Fine," Mason said. He dusted grass off his coat and

headed back to his brother, but as he passed Nina, she felt Manning's grip tighten on her arm. "Don't you touch me again," Mason said, pointing a finger. "Ever."

Pa's dark look kept her from unleashing any kind of rejoinder.

*P*A ROTATED HIS ANKLE. He beamed at Nina, eyes bulging with joy. "Right as a trivet," he said and laughed.

Jasmine, sitting nearby—and keeping Rachel close—spouted amen and smiled, while Father Mathias, sweating and noticeably tired, tucked his implements away. The priest's eyes were more sunken, crow's feet scratching at the edges. "Go easy though, Lincoln. That foot was badly turned. Give it time. Make sure it will support your weight before you go high-stepping with the lassies at the next dance house."

Nina snickered.

"You have my word, Father. And my thanks."

"Yeah. Thanks, Father," Buck echoed the sentiments, now standing and testing his leg, the wound nothing more than a dark smudge against his white skin. He had one of the Army blankets wrapped around "Little Buck" and the rest of his midriff, and Nina was amused by his pale legs. "I feel like dancing. Any takers?"

"You could use some fresh drawers first," Jasmine said, laughing.

"I reckon I could."

"And I happen to have some," said Pa.

Father Mathias put a hand on Nina's shoulder, drawing her attention. "You can do it too, you know. *Alignalghi.*"

Before Nina could ask what he meant by that, Strobridge wandered back to the group, scratching at his beard. "Healed everyone up, I see." He spread his hands. "Praise Jesus."

Pa stood, scowling along with Nina, Buck, Manning, Red, Jasmine, and Rachel at the railroad boss. "Amen," Pa said.

"Amen," Strobridge returned. "Look, I..."

Mathias raised his hand. "Let's not rehash."

The railroad boss sniffed and nodded. "Off to Galena then?"

"Red and I will abide by that decision for now."

"Me, too," Buck cut in. "Reckon it best we stay together for the time bein.'"

Manning turned to Nina. "Let's get some things together and figure out how we can carry it all."

Nina nodded and looked eastward and then to the south. The sun had warmed things up as it rode high in the sky now. These foothills were mostly scree and scrub, and she knew the footing would be unreliable at best. They'd be traveling through gulches, barrens, shrubland, and ravines. She peered southwest. The mountains from which they'd just come loomed, peaks jutting into the clouds like god killers, hills hiding what Nina worried might be an infestation of deaduns.

They'd be skirting those monstrosities in order to reach Galena—if they didn't kill one another first. Either way, they'd be hoofing it, and the way things had been going of late, she figured it was gonna be a hell of an expedition.

CHAPTER SIX

*T*HEY SPENT THE NEXT couple hours gearing up, putting together makeshift backpacks brimming with food and ammo, even gathering a rucksack of coal for campfires. Pa passed along most the duties, all of which were carried out urgently. Jasmine and Rachel remained inseparable throughout, wrestling over chores and fussing in a jocular way that Nina found a tad bit irksome. It weren't that she felt jealous or nothing. It just seemed out of place somehow, she reckoned. Maybe that's how they were dealing, though.

Or maybe what was getting to her was this *thing* she'd inherited, this power coming to life within her. A few days ago, she would have scoffed at such a notion, but now all

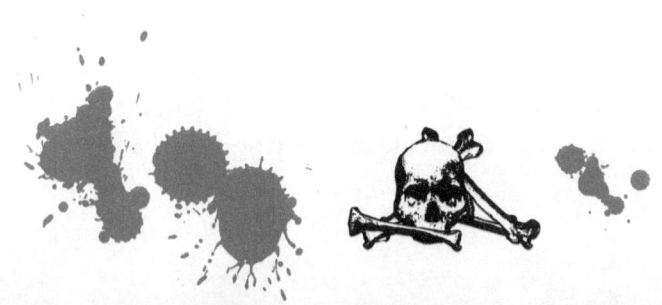

she heard were the sounds of the People, their drums and flutes, their whispers, words which began making sense on the fringes of her thoughts. All accept one. *Alignalghi.*

Nina was changing inside. The very thought rattled her soul.

On top of it all, the engine continued letting off smoke, reminding them that deaduns could turn up any moment. So they skinned out soon as possible, and the trip was made a little easier with Pa and Buck able to walk unassisted, even though George shuffled more than stepped, and Mason had to hang back and hold his brother's arm to keep him steady.

Nina walked alongside Manning most of the way, stealing glances, their hands touching on occasion. Strobridge and Father Mathias kept to opposite sides of the group, and Red Thunder scouted ahead. Buck and Pa didn't need help getting around anymore, but neither one could shoulder too much gear—two sacks each, lightly loaded with canned vittles and meat were all they managed.

A few hours in they had to descend a gully that ran more east-west against their general course, and then clamber up the far side, using their hands to ascend the steeper parts. Nina's legs burned and the day had turned warmer than expected, so she tied her shirt up to keep cool. She crested the top and sighed as a welcome breeze fluffed her hair and licked the sweat from her face.

Nina looked back at Manning and Red Thunder helping Rachel and Jasmine up, then she faced the sun, watched it dipping low, dying, painting the mountains blood-red and turning the clouds into strips of puffy, pink flesh.

"We gotta stop soon," Mason called out. He and his brother were the last to ascend, and they both looked done in.

No one argued. They were all dog-tired from the climb and another near-sleepless night. Even so, Nina felt reluctant to make camp. What then? Sleep? Dream about Liao's hell-fired devil train?

She glanced at her pa's makeshift boot as he and Buck conversed. Red Thunder had fashioned pieces of rawhide leather and canvas into a nifty piece of footwear, complete with eyelets for strings to draw the sides closed. It wasn't a boot, but Pa seemed to handle the hills and even the pointy rocks just fine.

"All right, we'll find somewhere suitable," Pa said, and he led them east, picking a path through slopes thick with mahogany and pines, so think in fact the shadows played tricks. Everyone was edgy and Nina's head ached from being all dried out and from eyeing every dad gum shadow for the least bit of movement. Several deer jumped up from the brush and she just about pissed herself. They were long gone before anyone moved again.

Pa finally found a creek bed and picked a secluded spot hemmed in by countless brown rocks that ranged in size from boulders to grit and some small pine trees. "Tricky terrain for any of them deaduns to cross without raising an alarm," Pa explained after Strobridge groused about "blasted rocks everywhere."

Coyotes began barking and yipping in the hills as Red Thunder built another one of his Dakota fires, this time letting Manning do some of the digging. The Indian worked untiringly with the kindling and wood until the deep bed of coal caught, producing a pleasant but intense heat.

"Gather around, ya'll," Pa called them in close. "Red's got

a daisy of an idea." The Indian then went over a series of whistles, teaching everyone signals so they wouldn't mistake each other for deaduns in the dark of night.

"Not sure how we'd get along without you," Pa said, shaking the Indian's hand. Nina saw even Mason Daggett giving a nod of respect at the native's skills.

With that, Red jogged off into the darkness, whether to keep vigil or because he found the coyotes more pleasant company, Nina didn't know, but she made herself feel useful by suggesting they scoop up pine needles and use them as beds to lay their blankets on. Jasmine praised her like it was the best thing she'd heard all day. Soon enough they all laid their blankets in a circle and began laying down head to foot.

Manning walked the perimeter on watch, a Spencer rifle in hand. Nina practically demanded to take second shift, but Manning shook his head. "You've done plenty," he said, giving her a dragged out smile as she stifled a yawn. "Just get some rest. Need you fresh tomorrow. Maybe you can teach me how to play that rhythm you were drumming up."

"Might require a private lesson," she said and, before he could get away, tugged his vest and kissed him hard, not giving a shit who saw.

That night, despite bedding down on pine needles and rocks, to Nina's great relief, she did not dream.

THE NEXT DAY, THEY HEADED SOUTH, becoming more emboldened by Pa's instinctive feel for the landscape. For someone who claimed not to know these parts he seemed familiar enough. "That chain's the Carson Range, and that one there is Sunflower Mountain," he said, indicating a massive snow-swept peak off to the west. "And the one behind it...that big one, that should be Mount Rose, and on the other side of it is the Tahoe Basin."

"And those there are the Painted Cat, the Shaky-Shaky, and the Big Nancies," George slurred, gesturing with his filthy hands as if squeezing a pair of tits. He seemed to be—unfortunately—recovering more of his old self as the day wore on. It had started with lots of confused questions, then complaints, followed by insults, and finally just his usual jackassery. "How far we got to go, old man?"

"My guess is we might make it to Galena by nightfall or before midday tomorrow."

"We *might* make it? Yer guess? He's just guessing," George said to Mason. Nina's pa was already starting to walk away, but George reached out and grabbed his arm. "Why we following this coot anyway? All you're doin' is *guessing*, old man."

"Turn loose of him, George," said Mason, but none too harshly.

"You know," George said, chin jutting as he swaggered closer to Pa. "You're lucky we never met in the field. I'd a gutted you like a pig."

"It's a good thing we didn't."

"Damn right it's a good thing."

Nina stepped up, her vision starting to go red again, and she noticed Mason took a step closer, too. If she had to go by the ears with both Johnny Rebs she'd do it and not hold back or *be* held back this time. "Let go," she said.

"What you think *you're* gonna do?" George scowled at her.

"Look, son, I didn't take any part in your war, so you have no reason to nurse these hard feelings," said Pa. "In fact, maybe you need reminding the war is done and over."

George Daggett's screw-mouth tightened up. "Over or not, you're lying. I remember you. I *seen* you. You was at Shiloh. I don't forget faces. You was at Shiloh, you fuck!"

"Let. Go." Nina said through grit teeth. "Last chance."

"Georgie…" Mason said.

Then Buck was there, too. "Why don't you back the hell up?"

"What? I cain't walk next to nobody? I cain't have a conver—"

"You need to back off," Buck repeated.

Nina noticed the big knife in his hand. Manning stepped up as well, hands resting on his holstered dragoons.

"C'mon, Georgie." Mason, seemingly too tired to engage in another round of threats, pulled his brother by the elbow. "You took a wallop during the wreck…and we ain't got the time for this right now."

"Everyone, settle," Pa said in a commanding tone. "George, I know you seen some bad things, and I don't doubt you saw someone that *looked* like me, but trust me, I was not at Shiloh nor any other battle in that terrible war. I feel for both sides. There weren't no victors. But we got to keep it together now. Things are transpiring all around us, and the real enemy is raising our friends and loved ones from the dead and turning them on us with their teeth and their fingernails, you understand me? We need to get to someplace civilized. Figure all this out. Your brother's right. We don't have time for this…." Her pa looked down at where George had hold of his arm, then looked back into the Southerner's eyes.

George sniffled and held Pa's stare for a long second,

then he let go. He looked around at everyone, all of them watching with various expressions. He looked at Nina, at Buck and Manning, past them at Father Mathias, Jasmine, Rachel, Red Thunder, and the shadowy figure of J.H. Strobridge, leaning casual-like against a tree. "Fuck all this," George said, then he turned and nearly walked into Mason, who grabbed his brother's arm to keep him from falling down.

"C'mon," Mason said, and led his brother away.

"I'll be glad to be done with those two," Nina said under her breath—once the Daggetts moved out of earshot.

Pa shook his head. "George is dazed and tired and feeling weak. And he's scared. We all are. If the world wasn't disorderly enough, now it's done gone every which way…" he peered at Nina. "And that keeps a man feeling all-overish."

"But not you, Lincoln," Father Mathias said, nodding at her pa. "You're a good man. A natural leader, and a keeper of God's peace."

"You do me too much credit."

"I don't believe I do."

"I'm glad you believe that, but you don't know me half as well as you think you do, trust me." Her pa watched after the two ex-Confederates for a second with a hard stare, then turned away. "Let's get moving."

NINA LINGERED BEHIND, WANTING nothing to do with the constant bickering. It was sounder with the Daggetts and Strobridge in front of her. Let Mathias, Buck, and Pa set the pace. All three got along just fine up there, and it served them well to put up a strong unified front so the Daggetts stayed docile. Nina preferred a stealthier vigil, and she drew Manning with her.

The fragile peace that had existed the day before seemed to be gone. The uneasy energy gave wings to their feet, as everyone seemed anxious to reach Galena, if only to untangle themselves from one another.

Half a day on, Pa pointed out Mount Rose was more westerly now as the group hugged the foothills while they ambled south. Nina gazed up at the tree-covered slopes and spiny Carson ridge to her right. The mountain range seemed peaceful, content, a monstrous wall of rock and snow that should have been a barrier between Liao Xu and the east.

If not maybe for the dad blasted rail.

Maybe those steel tracks *were* the catalyst that had brought all this on.

Maybe Liao was seizing his opportunity while the devils of industry gorged on the Land and the People, heads turned away as they gnawed and chewed and worried at the bone.

Maybe Red Thunder was right.

A slue o' maybes.

Dark clouds gathered in the west, squeezed beneath the sky's puffy white layers like grime beneath the nails, threatening to drop a funereal veil over those protective peaks. A low, rumble followed. Black thunderheads over top the mountains. Nina looked away. She'd enough darkness to last her a lifetime.

After another hour of plodding footsteps, the heat started its work. Sweat formed rivers inside her shirt, ran down her chest and stomach, saturating her clothing. Enveloped in her own stench, Nina kept her eyes focused on Jasmine's shapely brown calves as she walked ahead of her in the same filthy, torn dress she had on days ago when they'd first met. They'd have to get her some right proper duds for fighting off deaduns once they got to Galena and burn that damned, soiled dress.

Rachel called out, pointing.

As a group, they turned. Plumes of sooty gray smoke rose in the northeast, winding lazily into the sky.

Manning took off his hat and drug his arm across a sweaty brow. "What's that?"

"I imagine *that* would be Reno." Strobridge showed his stained teeth in what was either a grin or a snarl, then gave a nod. "Satisfied, Thomas?"

Father Mathias was coated in dirt, his black robes now more of a mercurial tone. "Satisfied? Yes. Happy? No." The priest turned and kept walking through the sediment and scrub.

Those poor souls in Reno were suffering the same harrowing nightmare now. It made the bile in Nina's stomach rise, but what could they do? What could *she* do? Nothing. That was the quick answer. So why did she feel a growing sense of obligation?

Nina sighed, irked at how easy her mind stumbled over the foolish idea of being some kind of a savior. She figured she could do with a distraction, so she unslung her pack and fished out an unmarked can and opener. The pack's hemp straps were burrowing into her shoulders, so she stretched her arms before she worked off the lid. Pears. Good. Nina loved pears. Could have been more beans, which were tasty going down, not so much coming back up later.

Is it sad, she thought, *that a can of pears is the high point of my day?*

She ate as she walked, using her knife to stab the dripping pieces of fruit, but as sweet as they were, her gaze kept going back to that dark column in the sky. She barely tasted as she chewed.

"Don't cut your tongue," Manning said, squinting. He brushed arms with her. "It just happens to be my favorite part of you."

Nina snorted. "Wait til you see the rest."

"You think maybe I'll change my mind?"

"This tongue of mine's nothing but trouble."

"I don't know about that. I fully encourage you talking. Every time you do, you either make complete sense or a damn miracle happens. So, no complaints from me. Not yet, leastways."

Nina soaked up his words, feeling more prideful than she had a right to. She pulled another chunk of pear and dropped it on her tongue. It tasted a little better. But she was curious about this Mister James Manning, and after these past couple days, she still hardly knew a thing about the man. He was about as tight-lipped as anyone she'd met, which, granted wasn't a whole heap of a lot. She and Pa never stayed in one spot too long. They had pretty much been on the trail for years.

"So where you from?" she asked. "And what brought you to Coburn Station? Or Truckee? Whatever the hell it was…"

James's face clouded over, mouth bending into a thoughtful frown. He kept his eyes pointed ahead.

"It ain't so hard, you know. Start with where you were born." Nina instantly regretted saying it that way. Maybe he *didn't* know. Maybe he'd had one of those tough kind of lives with memories best left buried and covered with a rock.

He chuckled, peered squinty-eyed at her. "I was born in Texas. San Jacinto Bay… Well, Galveston now. Changing from Coburn to Truckee is just following suit, I suppose. Names, they keep changing, eh, Ninataku? That how you say it?"

"Close enough. Go on. Don't duck the question."

He smiled, and through the dirt and scratches, his pearly whites made her smile, as well. "My daddy was a cavalryman in Sam Houston's army. He grew up in Kentucky and saw an opportunity to do something other than bag cotton, so he signed on with the Kentucky Rifles. He and my ma just been hitched. She was a nurse and forced her way onto the boat alongside daddy to help with whatever needed doing, stitching fellas up and the like. I was born in '36 the day after my daddy and his regiment captured His Most Serene Highness…"

Nina shook her head, having no idea what Manning referred to.

"A curly ol' Mexican named López de Santa Anna?" He chuckled—maybe due to her blank stare. "Old news. Not important," he said, checking the sky, then looking back at her. "Regardless, Texas became a U.S. State and eventually the American government rewarded my pa with a little over three-hundred dollars and an acre of land for every dollar for his part in the war." He held his arms wide and smiled. "So that's my story. More than you ever cared to know."

Nina chewed another sliver of pear. "I want to more about your ma. She sounds like my kind of woman."

Manning gazed ahead wistfully. "Ma did a lot of things. While daddy was off soldiering, she raised me and became a teacher and opened her own school. She was good with the numbers, too. Taught me how to work them. I had no brothers and sisters due to certain physical limitations. Her and daddy tried to give me a couple siblings, but they didn't make it. So, needless to say, I was fairly doted over."

"Didn't make it?"

"Stillborn."

"Oh." She'd had a brother born the same way, but she was maybe three and barely remembered it. Pa never spoke about it neither.

Nina tried to get an image of Manning's mother. Probably a willowy, female version of the man she was growing more attached to by the minute. She pictured a striking woman with sad blue eyes. "What did she look like?"

"Why are you so interested in my mother?" James looked bemused, but not in a displeased way.

"I lost mine," she answered, suddenly feeling the weight of it.

James touched her shoulder. "I'm sorry to hear that. I imagine that's why you and your daddy took to the trail?"

Nina nodded, but she wasn't prepared talk about all that right now. It was easier asking the questions. "Since you come from a soldiering family and can handle your iron, did you fight in the big war? You had to learn to shoot like that somewhere."

James shook his head. "No…no things got a little

muddled for me. My…*family*, they died of yellow fever, and I…"

She waited as he walked quiet beside her, deciding not to push him.

"Let's say I developed some mighty hard feelings against the world. Just had a heap of mean-spirited energy. And somehow, I don't quite remember, I fell in with some lawless types. Hardly even knew the war existed. Well, I *knew*… but I was too busy being a bastard, I reckon."

Nina let the silence ride out again, allowing her eyes to roam to her left over a set of low hills skirted by forestland. She believed that to be their destination and looked forward to getting there.

James laughed quietly. "Ma was pretty. Yes indeed. A head-turner. Her hair was gold and she had eyes like the clear blue sky. She had a strong Kentucky accent, but it was sweet and she loved to sing to me. Her voice, it made me feel…*safe*. I could have listened to her sing all day." He paused for a moment, seemed ready to continue, but stopped short.

"She sounds like she was wonderful."

He looked away, swiped a finger across his cheek. Nina presumed it was a tear, but knew better than to acknowledge it. James Manning was like Pa, and he wouldn't want anyone to think him weak.

"Thanks for bringing her up. Hadn't thought about her for a while, now. Good to take my mind off other things."

"What other things? Aside from the obvious, if that's what you mean."

"Ah," A raw expression touched his face and stuck there. "I took it out on Woodruff back there at the fort. I went hard on him. Too hard."

Nina wanted to tell him it wasn't true, but she couldn't. "Maybe he didn't deserve the beatin' you put on him, but don't shoulder the blame for it. Strobridge was the one made him into what he was. You were just…" Nina paused, trying to pick the right words.

"Too hard," he said.

"Well…" They walked on a bit in silence. Finally she said, "Seems to me there's something inside you. Something dangerous that…lies just below the surface. I'm wondering—"

Manning got a resolute look in his eyes. He stopped and looked at her, causing her to halt as well. "Nina, I never struck anyone without cause in my life." His blue eyes got intense, and his stare made her feel fluttery. "I'd *never* hurt you. Not ever. I'm on your side."

Nina nodded and let the understanding sink in, the pair of them going silent.

The men up front stood at the highest point of the incline, and her pa called back, "Everyone all right?"

Manning's gaze never left her. "We're fine."

"Nina?" Jasmine asked from twenty feet up ahead.

She glanced at the woman. Rachel next to her, both of them looking her way. "Everything's fine."

Pa was walking back their way, and she saw he was hobbling a bit. "There's a watering hole on the other side of this rise where we can wait for Red," he said as he got near. "We can decide if we're going to camp there or head on and try to make Galena before nightfall. Maybe Red's done some scouting further into the hills."

"Well, where exactly is this blasted Galena?" Strobridge

asked as he plopped down on the grassy ground. He looked a might bit topped out, not that Nina felt much sympathy.

Pa pointed toward the low hills and range of trees. "Should be around the left flank of those hills, to *our* right. We can hotfoot it over yonder in two, perhaps three more hours."

A half-hour later they rested at the edge of the watering hole, which was surprisingly large and still, with some toothy red and brown tufts of sedge here and there and small song thrushes chirping amongst the twiggy branches, pecking at the nutty seeds. George wandered up to the water, pulled his trousers open, and started relieving himself without so much as a *pardonne-moi*.

Manning stepped in between the Daggetts and the women, partially blocking their view. Nina reckoned it was more for Rachel's sake.

Buck was sitting on the rocky soil and emptying one of his boots. He shook his shaggy head as he looked at George. "Whole world to piss on and the man's gotta whip it out and piss right here in the water."

"I do have to go, too," Jasmine muttered low. "What about you, hon?"

Rachel nodded, then flicked a glance at Manning, her cheeks turning rosy. They wandered off behind some bushes, Jasmine turning and asking Nina if she was coming. She said she would in a second, but her feet had been throbbing something awful, and not just that but rubbed raw. She squinted at her bloody socks, then checked out the blisters on the outside of both feet by her small toes.

"I get mine on the heel," Buck said, and lifted the back of one callused foot. "What I would not give right now for a fresh *Palouse.*"

Nina nodded. "I'd prefer a wagon like the one we lost in Truckee. We had a pretty sturdy band wagon and a couple…a couple right smart Belgians…" She suddenly missed Apple and Oatmeal, and that supply wagon where she'd slept many a moon and felt safe and secure from the elements.

"Yup," Buck said. "Sure could use a bully ol' chuckwagon. What happened in Truckee with ya'll? You're peddlers, right?"

"Of a kind."

"Right. Ain't we all of a kind." It was more remark than question, so Nina just nodded as Pa walked over.

"How's about we open a couple of them cans?" he asked.

"Sure." Nina handed up her bag, but Pa didn't take it from her.

She peered up to see he was busy squinting elsewhere. Nina followed his gaze and saw movement in the tall grasses. Her thumb touched her holster, but then a familiar sight stepped into view. Nina realized every time she saw Red Thunder anew he was a welcome vision.

The Indian strode up and informed them there was no sign of deaduns or anything out of the ordinary, just a couple abandoned cabins in the woods and that was it. The decision was unanimous to push on straightaway, everyone agreeing there didn't seem much sense in braving another night outdoors if they didn't have to.

They quickened their pace over rangeland covered with bluebonnets and prairie-fire, dry shrubs and rough grasses, sometimes too thick or thorny, forcing them to skirt around. The land gave way to thick-limbed Joshua trees with their spiny leaves, white firs, copses of tough-looking pines, and other stunted desert flora. Red Thunder led them into a fertile valley, which wound around the base of the hills. Despite his scouting foray, they took extra care to keep quiet as they traversed the woods, rarely speaking.

Dogs barked, echoing hollow through the valley. They weren't coyotes but domesticated hounds, a sure sign that some type of habitation was not far ahead. The first steading they came to presented several buildings: a two-story barn with a fenced barnyard, a slant-roofed workhouse inside the fence. Beyond that was a pitch-roofed millhouse on stilts with odd stacks of cut lumber and felled timber hither and yon, and a big two-story homestead.

Nina heard a consistent chopping noise, and they rounded the barn to see a peculiar man splitting logs. Well, Nina thought it was a man at first, due to those heavy ax strokes inflicted on the wood, splitting them expertly each time, but the feller wore a calf-length twill skirt over boots and an ivory-colored bonnet. Then the 'man' noticed them, looked up, and presented a white woman's pale face, which turned sour upon seeing them.

Father Mathias waved, telling Pa, "You have the most likable disposition of us all, Lincoln. Mayhap you could talk to the lady?"

Pa nodded and straightened his shirt, took off his hat, and ran his hands over his hair. The wound on his scalp was nothing but a puckered line, like a scab that dried and healed up a week past rather than a wound taken just a day and a half ago.

The tall woman laid her ax on her shoulder as Pa took a step forward. Her ice-colored eyes regarded him with instant mistrust, and Nina noticed her thick-muscled sweaty forearms tightening on the ax handle. Atop her skirts she wore a dirty flannel work-shirt befitting any wood cutter. And, no mistake, she was a big girl. As tall as James and thicker—built like a goldurned tree trunk. She wasn't a looker, but weren't all that unattractive either, in a rugged-like way.

"Who are you, and what do you want?" she asked, her voice surprisingly high-pitched for her appearance, and also wary but unafraid. Her measured stare hesitated on Buck and Strobridge before moving on to the rest of them.

Nina peered behind them, then whispered to Manning. "Red's gone."

He gave a quick glance around. "No telling the attitude of folk around here."

"Ma'am," Pa nodded. "My name's Lincoln Weaver, and this here's my daughter, Nina."

Nina tipped her hat as Pa introduced the rest.

"I hope you don't expect me to remember all those names."

Pa smiled. "No, ma'am.

"Like I asked, what do you want?" Nina took note of the ax still gripped tight in the woman's hand.

"We've been hard pressed and we was wonderin' if this here's Galena and if you might know a place to stay? Or if we could talk to your pa about boarding with y'all for the evening? Maybe bothering you for a meal? We just come down from...north." Pa seemed to think carefully on what he was about to say next. He wanted to be honest, Nina knew, but also didn't want to spook the woman. "Our train derailed, and after trekking yonder wilderness we sure could use a good night's rest. We can pay for the inconvenience." Pa cast a quick glance at Strobridge, earning a grudging nod.

The woman gave them another thorough once-over, apparently unconcerned if she seemed rude. Strands of white-blond hair had escaped her bonnet, framing her cheeks and nose, but she didn't seem to mind. She was too busy passing judgment.

"Stay here. I'll fetch my pa." She turned and lumbered off, glancing over her shoulder once as she walked away, likely making sure no one was sneaking up on her.

"Why you out here choppin' wood when you got a sawmill right *there?*" George piped up. "Seems kinda boneheaded, choppin' wood when you got that there mill."

She stopped and turned, that hand squeezing around the ax handle. "I like splitting things in half, Mister... Daggett, was it? Ain't nothing I can't cleave with this old right-maker."

George laughed, genuine at first, then his joviality sunk like a stone under the woman's stare. She waited for him to say something else, but Mason, Buck, and even Strobridge told him to keep his trap shut, and the woman started off again.

Manning whispered to Nina, "She's a strapper. And handy with an ax. That's nice skill to own these days, you think?"

"If she likes cleaving things in half, she might get her chance sooner than later."

CHAPTER SEVEN

*T*HEY DIDN'T HAVE LONG to wait. Several folks came around the corner of the homestead with the big blonde woman in tow. Two men had slaverin' dogs straining at the ends of their chains, tugging their handlers along behind 'em. A man in a flat-brimmed hat led them, of medium height but well-stocky, decked in black trousers with suspenders pulled up over his white shirt. He walked with a cane to support what looked like a game right leg. Still, he outpaced the rest of 'em, and Nina wondered if he really needed that walking stick at all.

She counted five of 'em in total, including the two fellers with the dogs. They all looked a hodgepodge of ill-intent.

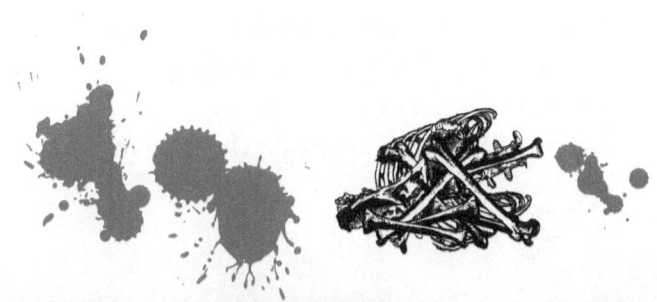

Among them came an immense, barrel-chested black man with a shotgun, a long-haired Mexican-lookin' feller with one of those growling hounds, and a lanky white man with a long beard handling the other beast. The dogs started barking and flinging strands of drool upon seeing them, and Nina and crew took a step back, wondering if they were about to get let loose upon. The man with the cane hissed over his shoulder, just once, and both hounds shut their slobbery yaps.

Pa smiled, acting unperturbed by the ominous bearing of the newcomers. "Fair amount of firepower you got there, mister. Understandable. We must have looked a fright to your daughter there, but unnecessary, I assure you."

The man stopped about ten feet from Pa, placed the tip of his cane in the ground before him, and leaned on it with both hands. Angling forward, he seemed to regard them through the top of his head, eyes darting around to absorb his surroundings. He *harrumphed*, then fixed Pa with a colorless stare. "That true what Greta said about a train?"

Pa nodded. "We had brake line troubles, hit a turn coming down the mountains too fast and derailed ourselves."

"Why didn't you go straight on to Reno then? What are you doing this far south?"

Damn, Nina thought. Pa trying to be honest only succeeded in him getting himself cornered.

Strobridge spoke up before her pa could reply. "To be honest, folks, it was bandits got us derailed. We were attempting to outrun them, and we feared walking the tracks into Reno with the culprits at our heels."

"We figured a change in direction might shake them

loose…" her pa added.

"Besides, our business is in Carson City," Strobridge continued, obviously seeing his opportunity to wrest control by bringing himself to the forefront. Nina did her best to keep the curl from her lip, noticing the big blonde called Greta was eyeballing her something fierce. "So we thought the safest route was to come on south through Galena. Not an easy walk to be sure, but we thought it best for our own safety."

The leader had narrowed his eyes as Strobridge spoke up, his probing gaze switching to the rail man. "And who might you be?"

"James Harvey Strobridge of the Central Pacific line at your service." Strobridge bowed. "We were on my private train coming out from Truckee when a clan of heinous bandits took hot to our trail. Men in ambush, on horses—"

Suddenly George piped up, "They even had another engine bearing down on us."

Strobridge cut back in before George screwed things up. "We're fortunate none of us were killed, although they did get all our precious cargo."

"That's unfortunate, Mister Strobridge. Sounds like you made the right decision to get yourselves away before more harm could come to you or the ladies. One's life is not worth any amount of cargo."

The man gave pause, burying himself in his thoughts. He didn't seem to mind how uncomfortable the silence got. He would make up his mind in his own time, Nina realized. He suddenly lifted his voice, tilted his head up a fraction. "Folks, my name's Jonathan Ramdohr and this here's my sawmill. You're welcome to stay for the night."

His men relaxed their grips on their shotguns, and Greta unwound those thick shoulders of hers, though her ax stayed put.

"Greatly appreciated, Mister Ramdohr," her pa said, talking over Strobridge.

The sawmill owner showed no sign of acknowledging Pa's thanks. "Now as you can see, I welcome all kinds: whites, Mexicans, Negros, even Injuns. I got no use for prejudice. And no need for money, neither. You pay your board by getting up with us tomorrow and helping with chores. We got fences need mending, stalls need cleaning, and if you know anything about debarking, planing, or edging wood, so much the better. If not, I can always use the muscle in the saw pit.

"Mister Strobridge, I extend the hospitality of my home to you in the sincere hope that it will be remembered as the rail system expands to fortify the infrastructure of this great country. I would like to discuss with you why you should consider a line to Virginia City and why we should be considered a part of that growth and expansion, if you please."

Strobridge bowed, his normally shitty grin seemed less shitty, and Nina figured it was his business smile and not its kin, the I'm-going-to-fuck-you-one-way-or-another smile. "Your hospitality is noted, Mister Ramdohr. The Central Pacific Railroad Company thanks you." No doubt, Strobridge's copper-laden pockets thanked him, as well.

"I'll have the men put the hounds away 'til you're settled in for the night. They *will* attack strangers, so do keep that in mind."

"Much obliged, Mister Ramdohr," Strobridge returned.

Nina watched Pa and Mathias look at one another and shrug.

GRETA RAMDOHR LED THE group past stacks of timber to a low building of workers' quarters attached to the back of the large, weather-worn barn. A pair of oxen watched disinterestedly as they passed by. She led them through a fence and to the stone workhouse with six doors facing into the work yard, which contained sawbucks and woodpiles, and a long table situated off to the side. Benches bracketed a well pump, and mounds of sawdust and wood shavings and a few buckets and barrels of tools were dispersed throughout. Pa was complimentary of the setup, and Greta nodded her thanks.

She gathered them near the table and gestured to the workhouse. "The three quarters to the left are yours. Divide them up however you want. Cato, Miguel, and Christopher been with us a long time. They got the other three. Wouldn't try to put 'em out if you know what's good for you." She indicated the pump. "You can wash up there. Dinner's in an hour. Mister Strobridge, if you'll follow me. You'll be rooming with us in the house."

"Ain't that some shit?" George Daggett shook his head.

The railroad boss patted George hard on the shoulder and chuckled. "Would look bad if I quartered with y'all lower types." He said it like he was joking, but Nina knew he full-on meant it.

After Greta and Strobridge departed, Pa took charge of the divvying. "I say give the ladies the outside room, Mason and George the inside. The rest of us will take the middle room." Pa looked at Buck, Mathias, and Manning. "Unless one of you cares to join the Daggetts?"

Manning and Buck looked at one another and both shook their heads.

George sneered. "Well, fuck ya'll, too."

"That's fine, Georgie," Mason said. "More room for us."

Nina, Jasmine, and Rachel took refuge, finding their room to be accommodating and clean, complete with two comfortable beds, some cups for water, and even a window looking out at a yard full of pines.

Jasmine shut the door and Nina melted onto one of the cots, unexpectedly relieved to be away from the men, and even more grateful Pa had chosen to put himself and Manning between them and the Daggetts. She sighed, slouched, and allowed the tension to roll off her shoulders.

"I hear you. All them men wear a girl out. You don't have to tell me. I been around 'em near twenty-four hours a day ever since I took up..." She glanced at Rachel.

The girl wrapped her arms around Jasmine and laughed. "Jaz, I don't give a fig you were some Calico Queen. You don't have to be sensitive with me. I'm big now, and my ma's gone, so I have to be tending to myself." The girl released her and sat down on the other cot, started to take off her boots.

Jasmine watched with an undecided smile.

"Sakes alive! Feels good to free these piggies." Rachel wiggled her toes, then cocked her head. "Jaz, what was it like?"

They'd been holding on to Rachel's innocence despite that it had been crushed out of the girl over the past few days. Jasmine looked at Nina.

Nina reckoned it was for the best Rachel Buell knew the

truth of the world. No more lies. No more sugar coating. Didn't matter no more she was thirteen years old. They were in this together. She gave Jasmine a nod, not that she felt like the woman needed her blessing or anything like that.

Jasmine nodded back at her, though, then said, "Well, like I was sayin', men, they will wear you out, whether they're humpin' you or talkin' your ear off. I learned to prefer the first. At least they're honest when they're having a go, plus at least you get *something* out of it—sometimes. But, Lord, everything out of their mouths afterward is just bluster, all lies and dreams that ain't never gonna come true." Jasmine sat down next to Rachel and looked at the floor. "Kinda sad really. And then, after they done talkin', they usually fall on back to their drinkin', yellin', hittin'…"

"So fucking is the safest bet?" Rachel asked.

"Girl, you shouldn't talk like that!"

"*You* just did."

"That's different. And I said 'humpin'. You ought not talk thataway."

"Why?"

"Well, because…"

"Because what? Because I'm white? I don't care what's proper anymore. Like I said, my folks are dead and gone. I can talk the way I please and to *who* I damn please. And right now I want to hear more about what your life has been like."

Jasmine shook her head and gave Rachel a hug. Then they started chatting about Jasmine's days of whoring—things Nina would have been shocked to hear a few days ago—while she removed her gun belt and pulled off her boots. She lay down on the straw mattress and Jasmine's and Rachel's voices became a low hum. The mattress weren't the most comfortable thing she'd ever laid on, but Nina was out before she could count to ten.

T HE WEIGHT OF SLEEP was so heavy she couldn't recall where she was or whose company she kept as she was shaken awake. Her hand shot went to where she always kept her knife, but it wasn't there.

"It's me," Rachel said. "Nina."

Nina blinked at her.

"Hi," Rachel smiled. "Come get some food."

The girl stepped out of the room, telling her come get it while it was hot and before the men ate it all. Nina shook her head to scatter the cobwebs. It was unsafe to sleep so deep these days. She'd have to figure out a way to be more alert.

Nina sat up, put her head in her hands, and took several heavy breaths to clear her mind, each one sounding like a forge bellows. The fog lifted as the moments passed, and she pulled on her boots. She threw a glance out the window. A casting of orange flickered in the dark outside, what Nina could only surmise was torchlight.

She got up, grabbed her gun belt and knife from the floor, and went out to the yard. Soon as she entered, the delicious smells of home-cooked chow nearly bowled her over. These kind of vittles she hadn't had in months and months. Her mouth went wet straightaway as she gave a quick look around. Manning, Pa, Mathias, and Buck sat at the table on a long bench, each with a heaping plate in front of them. George and Mason sat on the other bench.

"Nina, over here."

She looked in the other direction, to a long table laden with all the things she'd been smelling; bowls filled with potatoes and vegetables, a platter of beef, chicken legs poking up from a pan of gravy, and various side dishes the likes of which Nina had never seen. Behind the table, Greta kept vigil, whisking away empty dishes and bringing new ones out.

The big woman nodded at Nina, and she nodded back. Greta looked more feminine without the ax attached to her clenched fist. Jasmine, who had on some clean clothes—a cream-colored blouse and a plain black skirt—was loading up a spoonful of what looked like hot slaw, and Rachel, decked in a tan and rose-colored floral print dress with her hair pulled back in a bun, was packing a plate with a bit of everything.

Nina glanced at the men, shaking her head. "What happened to ladies first around here?"

Jasmine sidled over and bumped Nina with her hip, licking some gravy off her middle finger. "This is seconds for us." She smiled, apologetically. "Sorry we didn't wake you up. You looked so purty just a layin' there with drool hanging from your lip."

Nina grimaced and gave Jasmine a gentle shove. "Shut up, *Jaz*."

Rachel giggled and put a dripping chicken leg onto her plate, but then pushed it at Nina. "Here," she said. "This is for you."

Nina didn't argue. She thanked the girl and then covered everything on the plate with gravy. Greta, who had been watching with a bit of a frown, lightened upon seeing that and seemed pleased. The woman offered up a tankard filled with some sort of foamy beer. "We brew this here, my father and me."

"Thanks." Nina took a healthy gulp. It was cool, almost cold, filling her mouth with a bittersweet, honeyed flavor. "Jiminy! This is the best fuckin' draft I ever had."

Greta laughed then, and nodded her thanks.

Nina spent the next few minutes shoving food down, the men having given up the table. They stood around with their beers, talking or just enjoying the sounds of the night and being in a civilized place with nobody trying to shoot or bite 'em. At some point, Nina looked up to find George staring at her with that empty-headed look of his. She had some half-chewed potatoes in her mouth, so she pushed them forward with her tongue, smashing them between her lips in a gross display of etiquette.

George blew out with a bit of Southern scorn. Nina chuckled and went back to filling up, not caring if he watched her or not.

The night cooled, bellies began the arduous task of digesting, and light conversation started up. Pa and Mathias talked about the Bible, Pa rubbing his distended belly in contentedness. Manning marveled over Buck's massive gun, the rough-rider explaining why he'd designed it that way, and how he had to manipulate standard ammunition to get it to work right. Their voices drifted on the gentle breeze.

The table got cleared before any of them knew what was happening, and they were left with a small cask of the honeyed beer, which they did their best to empty. At some point, Mason Daggett disappeared, leaving George to stare off into the grove of pines just outside the reach of the torches, his back towards the group and a bottle of Kentucky whiskey they'd brought from the train between his legs.

A couple of hours before midnight, the hired men came out. The big black feller, Cato, waved and smiled. "Howdy. Thought we'd give you a little breathin' room before we bothered to acquaint with ya."

"Much obliged, Mister Cato," Pa said. "Have a seat."

The big guy sat down between Pa and Mathias while Miguel pulled up a stool near the edge of the torchlight and began whittling on a piece of wood. The tall white man, Christopher, engaged Buck and Manning about things like guns and news from the east.

Things were peaceful for a while, until Nina spied George, all screw-mouthed as he stared at the black man. It must chap his hide to see Cato sitting there so comfortably. At first George spoke more into his bottle, grousing and what-not, but soon he was airing it out a bit mouthier.

Jasmine eyed the situation, legs swinging from the table. "You see George being a fool?"

"I sure do, but he ain't got his big brother around. Maybe someone will kill him tonight." Nina was half-joking, but no doubt she was ready to be rid of George Daggett. She was wondering how she could have possibly felt any relief at all after Father Mathias had done his miracle healing on George a couple days ago.

"Should we say something?" Jasmine asked and sipped from her tankard, a thin line of foam lingering on her lip when she withdrew it.

Nina shrugged. "I say let's see what happens."

And in the next breath, it did.

Cato stiffened visibly, his eyes widening so the whites were starkly contrasted against his dark skin. The black man turned and gave George a hard glare. "What was that now?"

George hesitated, but then seemed to regain his courage. "I said we white folk are trying to relax and shouldn't have to bear the company of some uppity nig—"

The black man shot up. "Look here! I won't hear that word uttered around me. Mister Ramdohr wouldn't have it neither."

"That so, you fuckin' overgrown coon? You nuh-nuh-nuh..."

Cato blustered. "Don't say it. I'm a'warnin' you!"

George rose off his bench, tangle-legged and as beef-headed as ever. The Mexican named Miguel stood up, too, his knife still in hand from whittling.

"Don't say it or what? You gonna swing?" George spat. "What you think the Law gonna do about that, assuming you got *real* law in this no-horse shithole. Back home, oh, you'd swing alright—one o' yer kind brush a white man and they'd hang your whole damned coon-ass family."

Manning started to rise. "Look now, George—"

George adjusted his stance, stuck out his chest, and squared off with Manning. "You got something to say to me, *friend*? 'Cause I'll tell ya what, I've had enough of your shit these past few days."

Manning looked between the Southerner and Cato and settled himself. "You know what? Not this time. Go right ahead."

"Yes, go on, George," Buck added, then said, "We could all use some entertainment."

Nina noticed even Father Mathias was keeping mum, watching with his brows slightly furrowed in the middle.

Cato put his palm up to Miguel, and the Mexican gave a barely imperceptible nod. The black man—taller by several inches, broader by a country mile—looked down at George, and the Southerner gave a wobbly bow.

George spread his arms wide, spilling whiskey on the ground. "As you wish, my African king, lord o' the fuckin' jungle, ruler of apes and tigers and all kinds of weird jungle," he paused to blow a silent belch, "shit."

Cato stood stock still, so George stuck his face up, jutting his jaw out. "Okay, darkie, I ain't gotta say it 'cuz you know I'm thinkin' it, and you cain't do *shit about that*."

Mason emerged from the Daggett's quarters, buttoning his shirt. He stopped upon seeing the scene, smoothed his ruffled hair. Greta came out behind him, looking disheveled, as well. She still wore her dress, although her shirt was twisted and half fastened, and she held a shawl around her muscly shoulders. A cascade of blonde locks were loose from her bun and fell all about her face.

Nina and Jasmine exchanged a look, realizing where Mason had gotten off to.

Unabashed, Greta marched up and pushed herself between Cato and George, put her finger against George's chest. Nina noticed she was an inch or two taller than him as she scowled into his face. "You causing trouble?"

Mason gently—surprisingly so—intercepted Greta's pointing finger and eased her aside. "He's just a little roistered, that's all. Let's get you to bed, Georgie. That head wound has got you messed up, brother."

George tried to shove his brother but missed, nearly

plowing the ground with his face before Mason caught him. Once straightened, he bellowed, "I'll go to bed when I damn well please. Only me and the Lord know when that'll be, by God. Let me go!"

"I just had me a prayer meetin' with God, and he said now would be a good time." Mason patted him on the back and helped him along.

George's demeanor nosedived under the guidance of his brother. "But I'm comin' back to take that big bastard on, right?"

"Of course. Have us a good night's rest and we'll revisit it, what do ya say?"

"That's right. You always got my back."

"Always."

Greta followed the brothers to their door, whispered something to Mason, and then hoisted her skirts and hurried back to the farmstead without so much as a goodnight. The three hired hands retired shortly thereafter, Cato making apologies for any untoward hostility and assuring them he held no grudges against anyone.

Pa and Mathias retired next, shaking their heads about "that dolt," meaning George Daggett, and Rachel nodded off with her head pillowed by her arms on the tabletop. Manning, Buck, and Jasmine shared the last of the beer with Nina, making a few jokes and chuckling about Mason humping their host's daughter.

Finally, Buck drained his cup and said, "Too bad Red's not here. He'd be enjoying all this. He'd sure like this brew." He stood and stretched. "Want I should carry the girl to bed?"

"That's all right, Mister Patterson," Jasmine said, then

announced her exhaustion and woke Rachel, pulling her along with her to their quarters, and Buck headed off to his. Nina didn't miss Jasmine's wink as they went inside.

That left her and James. Alone.

"What a night." Nina sighed and stretched.

Manning stood and went for a beer, then sat next to her on the bench. "Turn around," he said.

"What?"

"You're tense. Turn around."

She did, wondering what he was all about, then he took hold of her shoulders, started rubbing and kneading her tired muscles. Nina stiffened at first as the rigid muscles refused to relax, but after a minute she had damned well melted into her seat. She nearly cried out when Manning's hands found a really sore spot, and she realized it was from when the deadun had nearly ripped her hair out, back during her rescue of the Buells.

Deaduns. She'd nearly forgot about them, or at least had wanted to, what with all the food and hospitality. Where were they now? What did Liao Xu have up his sleeve? When would he catch up with them?

Manning worked at the knot, drawing a wavering sigh from her and making her forget about that yellow-hooded, dark eyed sonofabitch and his walking dead. Manning's hands were...*incredible.* The further she slid into relaxed bliss, the more Liao Xu and his deaduns faded into tomorrow. If they *were* in Reno, they could all rot there, far as she was concerned.

Manning's lips suddenly tickled her ear lobe, making her shut her eyes and lean her head a bit. "I think Mason and Greta had the right idea," he said. "If the world's coming to an end, I want to spend whatever time I've got left with you, Nina."

"Ain't no one dying tonight." She stood up, took his hand, and led him out into the dark pines.

CHAPTER EIGHT

Nina fumbled with Manning's trousers as he backed her into a small clearing nestled in a grove of pines. He held her by the shoulders, smothered her mouth in a pleasant, suffocating way. Part of the difficulty in the trouser removal *was* his hardness. His penis stood up straight against his stomach, rigid as a tree limb, harder than she could have ever imagined. Hell, she'd not even seen more than a handful of peckers in her life—mostly accidental spottings—and she wasn't sure what to do with it.

Would have to figure it out as she went, she guessed.

But Nina knew enough about the basics of copulation to understand James being hard was a *good* thing, if a bit

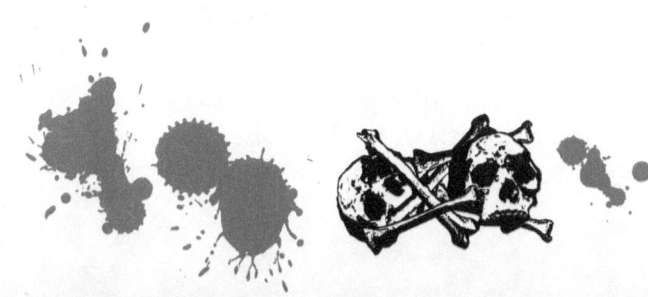

intimidating. They bustled and wrestled one another, fought their clothing free and tossed shirts and shoes into the brush. Before Nina could breathe twice, her holster and gun slid to the ground, denims right behind them.

A light breeze stirred up the forest, carrying the scents of bark and brush and dirt. His hands were all over her, leaving promises every place they touched.

"Wait," she said, stiffening, her hands rigidly pushing his away, fighting his advances even though she didn't want to. This was too much. She was too vulnerable.

Manning's hands stopped, but his lips did not. He kissed her neck, his breath sending chills across her shoulders. "I understand. It's too soon..."

But why resist this *now*? What was the point? Any thoughts about her safety seemed less important in light of the bigger cause; fears of disappointing Pa by impropriety or trying to live up to some false standard seemed silly. Hell, Pa *wanted* her to be happy. And he approved of James Manning. She could see it in his eyes. Something he rarely accorded to most folks. *Respect.*

In the end, Nina got the feeling she might be nothing more than a pawn. She'd likely have to sacrifice everything. So what harm did this moment bring? What great judgment on her soul? Nothing, was the answer. She gave in with a sigh.

Nina was curious about the tip of his cock brushing and bouncing against her quivering abdomen; she wanted it in her hand, to stroke it, to see what made James Manning tick. All that was left to do was to take it...

Hell with it, she thought, letting go of Manning's hands, in fact, *guiding* them to parts of her body she normally considered sacred places. His lips fell on her neck, kissing, licking, while a hand cupped her breast. She let out a long breath, and something more, something inside of her seemed to release and she felt free.

Not even layers of sweat-covered, blood-marinated skin could deter the man. Chills shocked her ceaselessly, heart pounding like a…well, like *a runaway train*. Manning put his hands between her legs, gently parting her. Nina's breath caught and she halfway climbed up his body from the pleasure, pulling one foot free of her denims and wrapping her leg around his waist.

Manning was a volcano, exuding incredible amounts of heat in the chilling air. But Nina burned, too, a firebrand of lust. She was dizzy with it, breathless, as he lifted her, carried her a few steps, and pressed her against the trunk of a large pine, the bark scraping at her skin. He started to enter her…

No. She slapped his chest with one hand and gripped his cock with the other, pushing him away and pulling him back at the same time. Even in the dimness she saw the fiery lust in his eyes…and maybe something more.

Nina turned around, pressed her shoulder against the tree, pushed her derrière against his hardness. It was all she could think to do after having seen Jasmine do the same thing with Strobridge. She briefly wondered if her legs were as long and inviting as Jasmine's, but no thought remained in her head long, not with the world melting around her.

Manning probed her down there with his fingers before something much larger replaced them. She spread her legs to accept it, gasping. Nothing she dreamed up could have prepared her for having Manning inside her. At first, it was an awkward, rough entry, despite his gentle attentions. He pressed down on her lower back, and she arched her behind upward. The angle allowed him to enter further. A sharp, quick pain in her abdomen followed that took her breath away as he filled her completely.

Nina strained against the tree trunk. "Oh *fuck*," she said, having no better words to describe the experience.

He stopped. "Are you okay?"

"Yeah…" She backed into him, filling *herself* this time, letting him know he didn't have to hold back. That she wanted it, too.

Manning took control, working himself into her and moving urgently. He reached around, fondling her breasts. An electric thrill tingled just beneath her skin, across her body, into her belly. Manning's thighs slapped against Nina's backside as she held on, her fingers digging into the scaly bark. Nothing could have prepared her for this. The hard pummeling against her bottom, Manning's strong grip on her shoulders, pinning her against the tree; opposite of pain, in fact, the most pleasant sort of contact. It was beautiful and violent all at once.

Nina's breath came fast, a shuddering built deep inside her core, wrapped itself around her and James Manning like a coiling snake. She'd thought herself a woman before, tossing a gun around and blowing deaduns to pieces, talking tough to ex-soldiers and rich railroad bosses. But this act had nothing to do with…*taking*. Or perhaps it did, only there was giving, too. Giving herself to a man. A man she… *loved?*

The word was sweet on her tongue, ready to slip loose. Then it was gone.

She smelled something, that *stench*, like a carcass left to rot in the sun. The shuffling through the brush, feet dragging, as telling as a lumbering heifer with a bell around its neck.

Still in the act, James unaware, Nina hugged the tree and peered around it, hoping to the spirits that it was Red Thunder and not what she feared. Then, from the gloom of broken-up moonlight, a man came shambling in the general direction of the barn. He was dressed in old trousers and a torn shirt that might have once been white but was now dingy and stained with gore.

The bastard was tall, his head brushed up against low branches. He gazed about, and with Nina's eyes grown accustomed to the night's darkness, she saw that roving dead stare and a gaping hole where his nose used to be. He made peculiar sniffing noises, the visible tendons on his face gargling these disgustingly wet, ticking sounds.

Nina's euphoria vanished, replaced with revulsion and a kind of heartsickness.

"James," she whispered. Manning hadn't noticed it, hadn't stopped humping her either. "James!" she raised her voice, regretfully pulling away from him.

"What's wrong—" He cut himself off. He'd seen it *now*. "Shh."

She felt him backing away, no doubt looking for his gun in the thick grass.

By sheer bad luck, the deadun stumbled in their direction, a stiff-legged, jerky gait, always on the verge of falling on its face but never quite managing the feat. It had either picked up their scent or its brain had told it to *go* at that particular moment. Who the hell knew?

Nina backed up, too, and used her feet to locate her holster. She stumbled, stepped on dry leaves and twigs. The deadun snarled, hunger in its voice, and altered its course, plunging at her around the pine tree. Nina had just enough time catch its slime-coated arms, one slipping free to grasp her shoulder with crust-hardened fingernails.

She let the thing spin her around, putting it between her and Manning. She had to keep those chomping teeth away from her vital parts. *Any* part, really. She'd seen what kind of damage they could do. Something else, too. The image flashed in her mind of Rachel's father, Grover Buell, turning into something horrid after being bitten by a deadun.

Nina kicked at its knee with her bare foot. It was a different affair without a boot and though the deadun's flesh and sinew folded away from its shin bone, she reeled off balance. It grunted and spun her around again, gaining momentum. A third time and they'd go down in a heap; she, naked, tangled up with a deadun. Not the most sporting of odds.

"James!" she cried out.

And he was suddenly there, bringing the butt of his dragoon down on the deadun's head. Nina broke free as the thing collapsed, making tacky *nap-napping* sounds with its lips. Manning stomped its head, while Nina desperately searched for her denims and holster. She spotted them and managed to get one leg in when more figures came bulldozing through the trees not twenty feet away.

She stooped and pulled her knife free, stepping out of her pants so she didn't get tangled. So be it—she'd have to fight unshucked.

The first deadun was a boy no taller than her shoulder.

Would have been nine or ten if he were still human and not a flesh-hungry biter. Since he was nearest, he'd be the first to go. She sidestepped as he darted in with a young yet feral growl and grit her teeth as she stabbed the boy through the eye, dropping him.

Part of Nina's heart turned cold; she knew they were just shambling mounds of flesh, and she'd put down deadun children before, but it still hurt her every time. It was something she decided she'd never get used to and would just have to take it out of Liao Xu's hide.

A gunmetal-hard anger was forming around her spirit, threatening to bury her in despair, for no one could be truly cold in their hearts without also being lost. The only thing to temper her frigid transformation was the warmth emanating from the spirit world, from the voices of the People, quite naturally a part of her now.

Together, the cold and heat forged Nina into a weapon. Was this part of the sacrifice she'd thought of only minutes before? Would she lose herself completely?

Two deaduns stomped through the scrub brush, arms reaching. They bowled each other over with their clumsy momentum. It was almost laughable if they weren't so goddamn gruesome.

Nina set upon them. She clutched one's hair and lifted its face up, exposing herself to its fetid breath. She buried her knife below the deadun's bony chin, pulling it out along with a gout of thick, gluey blood. She let go and its head flopped down, then she backed up and coaxed the other one to her. "Come taste my knife, you shitbird."

It rose, moaning "*erheee!*" to the moon. Black sigils suddenly pulsed across the skin of its forehead. It began to change, jelly-white eyes filling with spectral darkness, teeth chattering together like it had some kind of deadun flu.

He was coming. *Liao Xu.*

"Goddamn scouts," Nina said.

Before the change could finish, she flipped her blade so the tip pointed down, held it two-handed as high as she could, and brought it down with all her might. The knife slammed into the top of the deadun's head, sinking to the hilt, jarring her shoulders in the process. It fell against her and then down, dragging itself across her gore-soaked breasts and leaving bits and pieces of itself behind.

Nina stepped back and pushed it to the ground before searching for other deaduns in the vicinity. There were none. Then she saw Manning, his shirt hanging open and belt buckle hanging loose, standing and staring at her, the still form of a deadun sprawled in a thorny bush not far from him. He seemed to be suppressing a chuckle.

"What?" she panted.

Manning shook his head. "I'm not sure why…I mean you're covered in blood *again*, but…you are one beautiful woman."

His words disarmed her. She wanted to grin at him, but she steeled herself against his unanticipated flattery, saying, "That one was turning."

"Turning? You mean, like, changing?"

She nodded, still looking around and trying to catch her breath.

"Into what?"

"Hell if I know," she said. "Liao Xu, I think."

James nodded. "Makes sense, I reckon. We know he can do it. He's huntin' us. You think he saw you?"

"I don't know. But I do know I'd like to get my britches back on."

"Hold on. There's thorns and who knows what all around here. I'll fetch 'em."

Less than a minute later, Nina had her shirt and her denims back on and was buckling her holster when another chorus of grunts and wet gurgles came from somewhere not too far away.

She and James looked at one another, their eyes wide. She bent and pulled a boot on. "Damn it…"

"They must be trackin' this way," Manning whispered. "We need to warn the others."

A whistle cut through the night sky.

"That's Red." She hurriedly yanked on her remaining boot.

"Good," James said. "He must have discovered them, too."

Suddenly Ramdohr's dogs started barking their heads off from somewhere past the barn some forty yards away. The mill boss must have let them out once his guests settled in. She hoped that was in their favor, trusting the dogs would be more likely to go after deaduns than her or James.

Something tore through the ring of brush and thorn. James turned as the deadun loped at them, giving a throaty hiss as it attacked.

"Don't shoot it. You'll draw the others."

"I'm *not*." James ran at it just as it ran at him. They came together, a scrunching of grass, grunts, a *thwak*, an exhale of air, then something tumbling to the ground.

"I hate treating my guns like this," he said. "C'mon. Let's scoot."

"I need my hat."

"Nina, we're gonna have a herd of dead, hungry bastards on our hands any second."

The sounds of deaduns crashing through the brush grew louder, their groans and grunts like a muted stampede. It could have easily been a herd of cattle. Only cattle didn't stink like that. Not exactly.

"Damn it, Nina. Couldn't you have kept your hat on? Why'd you leave it?"

"Sorry, James. I ain't never been fucked in the woods in the pitch fuckin' black before. You were my first."

Manning kicked at something in the darkness. Whatever it was hit the ground hard, and the wet thuds of right good skull-pounding followed. There was a pause.

"Sorry," he said. "Just don't want you to get hurt. At the same time, I realize a woman takes her time. Ain't my place to tell you that."

A grin broke across her lips. Manners all day, displayed even at the worst possible times. But he was right. They needed to get the hell out of here. Nina was just about to abandon the search, when she found her hat on the opposite side of the pine tree about six feet from where they'd been copulating.

"Got it," she said, and they started running north towards the barn without looking back. The stench of the undead faded, but it wouldn't last long. The deaduns were coming.

They broke into the yard and were met with complete silence. The doors to the quarters were all closed. Not a single person stirred.

"Everyone was shit-faced just an hour ago," James said.

"No wonder they're not up."

"Pound on the doors. You take the near end, I'll take the far." Nina said, going to the sawmill workers quarters, glancing over her shoulder as she did so. Red Thunder jogged out of the gloom, his bloody tomahawk in hand, and she felt an instant sense of relief...then hoped for some reason he hadn't seen her and James in the woods having a go at it.

Cato, Christopher, and Miguel came warily out of their rooms; Cato with a shotgun in hand. "What's wrong?" the black man asked her.

"Just come with me," she said and went to join the emerging group.

Everybody was coming out piecemeal in various states of undress. Jasmine looked at Nina and got the hint right away; she went back inside and returned with a Spencer and ammo. Pa and Buck were already armed, although Buck was shirtless and looking like a sleep-eyed grizzly with all that daggone hair.

The brothers were predictably grumpy. Greta was nowhere to be seen.

"What's going on?" Mason asked.

"That's what we'd like to know," said Cato, keeping his shotgun at the ready. Miguel and Christopher were a step behind him, one to each side.

"Deaduns in the woods and coming this way," James said. "Load up."

The three mill workers looked confused, and then Christopher spotted Red Thunder lingering behind Buck. "Injun," he hollered and pointed.

Cato raised his barrel. "Someone better explain what

this Injun doin' here. He wasn't with you last night. Y'all thinkin' of robbin' Mister Ramdohr? Cuz if you are, tell me now and let's have it out."

Nina stepped in front of Red, spreading her arms wide with her palms up. She wasn't sure her actions wouldn't get them both killed, but on the other hand, she'd looked down plenty of barrels lately. She wasn't backing down from these fellers. "He's one of ours, but nobody's planning to rob anyone. You have way worse than that to worry over, trust me."

"Always making friends, Red. I wish I had yer magnetism," George said, while his brother disappeared into their room to retrieve their Spencers.

Pa pushed passed Buck and Father Mathias to stand next to Nina. "This here is Red Thunder, and he's on our side."

"Where was he when y'all came upon Greta and Mister Ramdohr?"

"You know as well as I that folks are trigger happy these days when they see a native; so instead, he's been out scouting the surrounds. Probably discovered the deaduns and is coming to warn us, ain't that right, Red?"

Cato looked confused. "What you mean *deaduns?*"

"You wouldn't believe me if I told you. Just know that everyone's lives are in jeopardy, even Mister Ramdohr. We got a fight on our hands, and y'all best go fill your pockets with shells."

Cato lowered his barrel. "You seem a good man, Mister Lincoln, and ya'll have a man of the Lord with you, so we'll fight to protect our own, if we got to."

Mason came back out and tossed his brother a rifle.

"Well, you got to," George said as he cocked the Spencer and loaded a round in the breech block by pulling down the lever and snapping it back up.

"We got the magazines," Jasmine called over. "Bring us all the loose ammunition." She and Rachel had been busy gathering the Spencer tubes and various pouches and weapons, sorting them on the long table. "Rachel and I wi—"

The first of the deaduns breached the tree line, hissing.

The whole swad of 'em had been rambling forward at a decent pace, and now here they came in quickened, stiff-legged gaits. Milky orbs rolled in their heads, and their noses twitched. A motley chorus turned Nina's gut; squeals and urgent simpers, gurgling whines and whoop-like coughs—deadun intellects all expressing their insatiable hunger.

Cato and Miguel gaped, while Christopher quaked in his boots and made the sign of the cross. Nina shook her head, not because she mocked the man's faith, but because of their priceless expressions. She and the others were long since beyond that stage.

Nina gave Cato a swat on the shoulder. "You think they look bad. Wait till you smell one up close."

Cato's teetering sanity seemed to be playing out across his face, and Nina knew he had to say something to make sure he hadn't just gone plumb crazy. "What…what…?"

"That's what we call deaduns."

"How long you been…" He couldn't take his eyes off 'em. "You all been running from these things?"

"About four days now, give or take some hours. My account of time's been kind of mucked up a bit lately."

"Where they come from?"

"I'll tell you what," Manning said from just on the other side of her. "Worry about making it through this. If you're still around later, we'll have a few of those beers and talk about it." Nina could hear the strain in James' voice, and she hoped it wasn't because he thought he needed to protect her.

She picked out the first line of targets, remembering what they'd talked about on the walk there. "Couple things, fellers," she told the sawmill workers. "Call 'em out if you can. Go deep. Shoot 'em in the bean. Best way to conserve ammunition, and the only way to take 'em out without a scuffle."

"That it?" Cato asked.

"That's all you need to know."

"Ignorant-ass neck-tied cocksucker," George Daggett called out from the center of the line, dropping the first deadun.

Nina shrugged, scanned the shambling crowd. "One-armed, red-haired beauty," she shouted, dropping a young, snarling woman she thought might have been stunning when alive.

Shouts and gunfire erupted all around, once again delivering that ceaseless ear-pounding only a hail of lead and black powder can make. Her nose itched almost on cue, and she rubbed it to avoid a sneeze.

Several days of grave rot had made many of the deaduns indistinguishable from one another, but others had something Nina could speak on, something that set one apart from the others. Even so, it was often too loud to be heard over the guns, but calling them out was a way to make the process of mowing down biters a little easier. Kept the panic from taking hold.

Nina found one such target and named her. "Bonnet lady!" She promptly removed the woman's hat with a drop of lead.

With nine guns blazing, deaduns stumbled forward and dropped just as quick. Still, some got through, and the yard began filling up with those fortunate feeders, some missing a considerable percentage of the flesh they'd originally brought with 'em by the time they made it halfway across the killing field.

Father Mathias bolstered the line with his preaching, holding his Bible high, slinging verses like whitewash against the undead horde.

Nina exchanged a magazine with Jasmine and resumed her position.

The priest's invocations affected the deaduns in the most miraculous way. The majority fetched up cold where they stood, unable to move another step because of something in Father Mathias's words that kept them at bay. Still they hissed, snapped, and caterwauled at missing their chance at a meal.

"Hold!" Buck shouted. "Hold!" The firing stopped, and they waited a moment to ensure the deaduns were indeed stuck. "Okay, folks. Save your bullets. Let's knife 'em."

Nina put down her rifle and waded into the sea of frozen flesh, Red Thunder at her side. She picked a victim, some nameless man whose eyes rolled at her as she approached. Knife point to its throat, she slammed her right palm against the hilt, drove the blade up into its brain. Nina was rewarded with a burst of rot-thickened matter, like popping a sore. It gushed warm over her hands, oozing between her fingers.

Over and over, Nina slew what was already dead. A true angel of death, she never missed. It was a bloody business. She knifed a dozen of them or more. Her hands throbbed, blisters springing up where her knife hilt rubbed her palm raw. She glanced at Red Thunder who had a much simpler approach; tomahawk to the top of the head, spilling brains everywhere. Nina had reckoned she was beyond gagging, but the sight of Red's handiwork nearly made her upchuck.

Ain't no blasted way, she thought, and forced her gorge down. That meal was too damned gratifying to let loose.

"I'm sorry, friends," Mathias said, his voice sounding weak. "I can't hold them any longer. My faith is...lacking today."

"Today?" George scoffed. "Yer faith sure got a way of runnin' out on you, Padre."

Nina and Red Thunder returned to their positions after having taken down forty or fifty of the stiffened corpses. Nina was proud. That was a hell of a lot of ammo saved.

"We got a secondary plan?" Pa lifted a pistol and dropped a deadun waking from Mathias's spell. "Doesn't look like Liao's gonna run out of bodies anytime soon. Must have sent all of Reno to our doorstep."

"There's only one plan," Mason shouted. "Shoot till you cain't no more, then run so you can do it again."

Buck tripped a deadun that walked right past him, headed for Jasmine. "What gave you the impression there was a place to run?" he yelled in Mason's direction, then crushed the back of the deadun's head with a rifle butt.

Nina hefted her Spencer, wincing as more deaduns

filed into the yard, crawling over the bodies they'd already dropped. She shook her head. That hemmed-in feeling, like back at Fort Bluff, returned full force. "Liao Xu is coming after us. You know that, right, Pa?"

"I know, darlin'. For whatever reason, he's got it in for us. And we'll be back to axes and knives soon."

"What do we do then?" Cato asked. The sawmill workers looked exhausted, mentally more than anything, their eyes still unbelieving, their hands trembling on their weapons.

A razor shriek cut the night sky. Nina instinctively dropped to a knee, her shoulders hunched protectively, thoughts of those devil crows in their multitudes. The tumultuous sounds of flapping wings descended as everyone looked up.

"Holy Christ!" someone yelled, and Nina heard Rachel scream as a massive shadow fell from the sky.

CHAPTER NINE

*S*OMETHING WITH HUGE, BLACK wings swooped down over their heads. The sawmill worker named Christopher fired his shotgun skyward and screamed as talons snatched his shoulders. Man and beast struggled. Christopher stomped and cursed, trying to get the large, feathered thing off him. The creature raked pieces off the man—shirt, hair, and skin went flying, spatters of red exploding—as he spun in their direction, shotgun swinging wildly back and forth, up and down.

Nina hit the deck, saw James and her pa doing likewise. Most folks stood gaping, though, at the sight of the strange creature. The shotgun went off, and Miguel's left arm

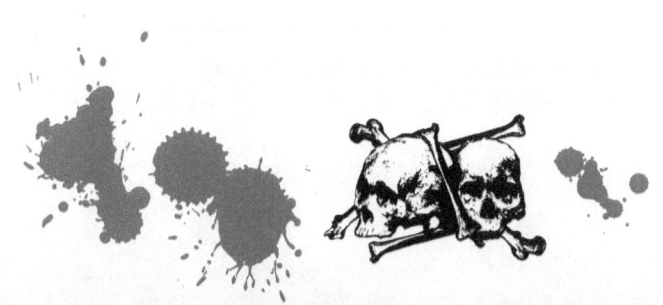

disappeared, his torso peppered with shot. The Mexican screamed and collapsed.

Nina tried to draw a bead on the flying thing when Christopher's head just popped loose from his body. It arced through the air, long beard trailing like a mule's tail, and *thunked* on the ground near her feet. The winged shadow beat its wings, kicking up dust and straw, as it carried what was left of the man into the sky.

"Shit! *Fuck!*" George cried.

"That about sums it up," Mason said.

"What the hell was that?" George looked agape at the sky where the thing had disappeared.

"We got other things to worry about right now!" growled Buck, his modest gut bulging over his belt, weeks of road-dirt and deadun gunk having turned his skin a mottled, sweaty brown. He slapped the cylinder shut on his huge pistol after having reloaded and put a slug in one of 'em getting too close, blowing its open-mouthed skull to bits.

Nina stood, sighted, leaned into the stock of her Spencer, and dropped two more deaduns, brains and hair and eyes flying into the pines with wet splashes. She looked around for Cato.

The big man had pulled Miguel from the front line and placed him against the workhouse wall. His gun leaned there, too, and that was one less used against the deaduns. Cato held a handful of Miguel's entrails, loopy strands like a bag chock-full of snakes, and tried in vain to keep them inside even as they slid between his fingers. Blood poured out of the Mexican's stump, and his skin was gray.

Cato mumbled, "Oh, Lord. Oh shit. Oh *shit*, Lord. We're in some *shit*."

Nina's heart went out to the man, but she couldn't spend time worrying about it. She held the left flank now by herself, and deaduns were closing. Nina hunched over her Spencer, eyes glancing at the sky.

George echoed her sentiments. "We ain't doin' shit with that goddamn thing flyin' around up there!"

"I'll drop the bastard." Buck searched the darkness, determinedly poised, his monster pistol at the ready.

"Get it," George shouted, surprising encouragement coming from the Rebel. "I'll cover ya and keep killing these bastards."

Pa and Manning shouted an exchange, James yelling the news to her. "Nina, we're going to make a break for Ramdohr's house."

Nina nodded, a tremble rattling her as the flying thing's shriek split her ears. Beating wings sounded overhead. She ducked her head, glancing up, then dodged a grabbing deadun and walloped it with her rifle butt. With that damn thing in the sky and biters all over, making a break for it might not make much difference.

The deaduns kept coming into the work yard. They'd knocked over pieces of the fence facing the woods and pressed in through the gaps, sacrificing their flesh for those who came behind. Their bodies piled up, death in mounds of putrid, twitching flesh.

The shadow swooped back down again. Nina dropped, feeling the air curl around her head as it soared by, her butchered locks whipping. Missing her, the thing lifted and dropped again, putting those clutching talons into Red Thunder.

Nina's stomach dropped, knowing what that diabolical

thing had done to Christopher. She couldn't lose Red Thunder. She tried to get a bead, as the Indian grasped at a greasy-looking, taloned leg and swatted it with the business end of his tomahawk, cutting huge, licorice-colored chunks from it. The thing shrieked and released Red, flapping its wings with frantic intent as it aimed for the sky. Buck's gun went off, and the leaking bird-thing fluttered madly toward the pines, crashing amidst the branches.

"Ma'am!" someone yelled.

It was Cato, and she didn't have to look to know his words were a warning. She backed up and barely avoided a swiping hand belonging to a one-armed deadun. It staggered, and a second bony biter with frizzy white hair and a blood-soaked gown bustled around it, leading with its snapping jaws and a mouthful of black, broken teeth.

Nina stumbled, fell into Cato. The big man pulled her to her feet with one arm and cracked the white-haired deadun with his shotgun barrel. Nina charged the one-armed biter and smashed it in the head with the butt of her Spencer. Instead of going down it slavered and hissed, so she spun the barrel around. She'd lost track of how many bullets she had left, but pulled the trigger anyway and her piece fortunately lit the bastard up.

More piled in on her and Cato, cutting off their escape route. She looked for her pa and Manning, picking out the flash of James' gun. He was embroiled across the yard, a score of deaduns between 'em. Three or four snatched at her as the black man beside her bellowed and swung his emptied weapon. A deadun grabbed hold of the shotgun barrel and they started tugging it back and forth.

Grabbing hands and gnashing teeth blocked her view.

Nina pulled the trigger, but this time got a hollow *click* in response.

"Shit!" She threw the Spencer at the deadun and pulled her knife. Her stomach churned with panic, but she forced it down as best she could. Allowing fear to take hold meant hesitation, and hesitation meant death.

She caught a glimpse of Pa, James, Jasmine, and Rachel as they fled the work yard, whereas here she was trapped down at the far end. Over the gunfire, yells, and moans, she could hear Pa hollering her name.

"I'm comin'!" she hollered in reply, but he couldn't hear her.

It's all right, she thought. *Keep your wits.*

Nina told herself she was not alone. Her brothers and sisters encouraged her from the Shadow Lands, their song a slow and purposeful hum, giving her faith when others might have long ago become paralyzed by fear. She wouldn't die here. She wouldn't allow it.

A feral cry escaped her lips, and she dove at the oncoming wall of flesh. Like a snake, her knife bit, and she shoved inanimate bodies away, dropping them and creating a barrier of dead and rotten flesh two or three deaduns high.

Cato almost got his ass stabbed as he stumbled into her—she'd plumb forgot he was still there. She held her knife thrust, glancing at the dull, general purpose knife in the big man's oversized fist. Standing together, his blade was a couple inches shorter than hers; she couldn't help but chuckle.

"Trade me?" The big man said and *grinned*. Nina found it a surprisingly comforting expression in all this slaughter.

She shook her head and flashed a grin back. "Just do as I do."

"I'm a'doin'."

Separated from the rest, it was time to fight for their goddamn lives.

Despite his sweet demeanor, Cato was an awesome brute, his style simple and effective. He held his knife in his left fist, raised it to his chest in a reverse grip, and folded his right hand over top in a two-handed grasp. He roared, and from the corner of her eye, Nina saw him nearly decapitate a deadun with a powerful downward swing to the throat. His dull blade slashed through its neck in a splatter of yellowed bone and gristle.

Soon they'd cut a swath through the moving flesh, shielded by the growing wall of putrid dead on their left. Nina got an idea. A longshot, but wasn't everything a longshot these past few days?

"Stack them against the wall."

"What?"

"I said, stack them, damn it, against that wall!" She pointed.

Light dawned in Cato's eyes, and he tucked his knife in his pants. By this time, his shirt had been ripped free by clawing deaduns, and his dark skin glistened and pulsed as he went to work, pulling bodies even as Nina laid them out.

After what seemed like an eternity, although Nina knew it was only a minute or less, Cato said, "All right, miss. I hope this works!"

Nina didn't even turn. She had her eyes on a group of deaduns not so fresh from the grave. They had a dusty look about them, held together by little more than sinew.

"Go then."

"Ladies first."

"*You* first. If it'll hold you, then it'll hold me. Now get up there. We ain't got time to argue."

The big man grunted, and the wet sounds of his climbing reached her ears. Bones crunched, presumably beneath Cato's bulk. She thought she might have heard him retch at some point.

Nina carved up two of the old timers, dust-choking snappers, with their mummified flesh pulled tight across their faces. Was Liao running out of fresh bodies?

Just when Nina thought she'd never hear from Cato again, he shouted, "I'm up! Hah! Lord be praised! Come on!"

Nina reached deep, dragging her resolve from the shadows, searching for something to kindle the fire of her spirit. She remembered Red Thunder's words; she only need let the People in, to feel them in her soul, to become one in spirit. But how would it affect her? Would she lose a piece of herself? Would she still be Nina Weaver? The strong, independent part of her resisted. She'd already given herself to James Manning, and she trusted Jasmine with all her heart. Wasn't that enough?

No. The voice of the *boha gande* spoke inside her. *Ninataku, you have, and always will be at one with the People. They will always love you, surely as the sun rises every morning. Life is about bravery and strength, yes, but it is also about letting go. Let go. There is nothing to fear.*

Nina sighed, removed all the barriers around her heart and mind. She exposed her spirit to her brothers and sisters among the Shoshone.

Defend your daughter, she asked them. *Touch my spirit. Help me.*

A wind filled her lungs, some gust from the Spirit World. A high-pitched *aieee* tore from her throat, a war cry from the other side, something akin to what Red Thunder had issued when attacking Liao Xu back at the fort. Nina imagined she could crack the earth with such a call, her voice a hammer in the hand of gods. The sound drove her forward into the deadun ranks, kicking, stabbing, knocking them down, buying time.

When she thought she'd created enough space, Nina turned and sprinted for the pile. It was a four-foot mound of twisted, bloated carcasses. Stomach's popped with oozing gasses, tongues lolled from crushed mouths. Their sightless eyes bulged, staring up at the glaring Sierra Nevada moon.

Cato stood on the worker's quarter roof, squatting down, both hands open for her. If she could just make it...

Nina hit the pile running, one boot finding purchase, then sinking as part of a deadun's chest gave way. Her other boot caught and slipped too, traction fleeting beneath her heels. She stormed up the pile, barely gaining ground.

Nina fell forward, her hands in it now; her fingers brushing exposed bone, poking soft, wet places, sinking into squishy cavities, and clutching limbs covered in viscous slime. Nina kept her head up, eyes on Cato.

"C'mon! You can do it!" he encouraged her.

At the top, she stretched, but remained a good ten inches short of the big man's grip. Her other hand slapped against the edge of the splintery roof but she hadn't the strength to pull herself up. A deadun beneath her slid sideways, and Cato grabbed for her and missed. Nina found purchase on another corpse, jumping as best she could on the soft flesh. Cato squatted further, grasped, missed again.

For a brief instant, Nina thought about turning and taking her chances with the biters. Could she somehow carve and dodge her way out of this mess?

No. She'd give it one more try...

Nina leapt again—feeling deadun hands grabbing at her feet now. A stilled biter rolled off the pile beneath her, and she knew there was nothing left beneath her feet to land on. Cato knelt and stretched. Nina's fingers wiggled for something, *anything*...

The big man's hand clapped over her wrist, enveloping it in his grip.

He hoisted her up and up, out of the yanking hands of deaduns below, her stomach and legs scraping against the edge of the roof, splinters of wood clawing at her skin. She landed atop Cato, sprawled across his bare chest. Without thinking, Nina took the man's damp head in her hands and kissed his sweaty forehead.

Cato looked more terrified of Nina than he had of the deaduns. "Now, miss, that ain't..."

Nina picked herself up and offered her hand. "Shut up. That was a thank you."

"Yes'm." Cato took her hand but helped himself up mostly; there weren't many men, oxen, or mules capable of getting the huge fellow to his feet if he didn't oblige, figuring he had to be all of three hundred pounds.

Still flustered, Cato led Nina across the low quarter roof, which butted against the barn. A ladder hugged the far wall.

"This go to the top of the barn?"

"Yes, ma'am."

"Can we get down the other side?"

Cato nodded. "We can, just be careful."

Nina went up the ladder in seconds, suddenly finding herself perched on a perilous incline. She took two steps and froze, Cato's warning sinking in. Her boots barely gripped the wooden shingles, and she could feel the smooth, weather-worn dryness. A faint wind buffeted her. What if she fell? Must be a thirty-foot fall. Nina pictured herself sliding down the overlapping slats to be summarily dumped into the horde of deaduns below. Or worse, what if there was another of those *things* flying around? The roof had been a good idea when she first thought of it, but now she wasn't so sure. She pitched herself against slanted surface, one hand clinging to the peak.

"Miss."

"What?"

"Ain't nothin' to be scared of. Watch me."

Nina opened her eyes a squint and watched Cato climb up the two or three feet to the top. He stood with one foot on either side of the peak and smiled down at her, squatted and offered his hand. "I done this a hundred times. Just like you done that down there."

Nina nodded and took the rough, work-hardened hand and allowed herself to be pulled up. She stood easily with Cato's support, surveying the scene. Deaduns swarmed out of the pine forest behind them, staggering through the moonlight. There were so many.

But no sign of her friends.

"Let's go before they get around the barn."

Cato led Nina across the roof. Short, shallow breaths and counting steps got her across. At the far end, Cato pointed in the direction of the house.

"Someone made it. See them lanterns?"

Two or three lights bobbed on the long porch around the front of the house. As they watched, gunshots flared in front of the lanterns. Folks were alive over there and making a stand, but that meant the deaduns were coming from elsewhere, too.

Cato shimmied down the roof a pace and spun onto a ladder ascending the front of the barn. Nina followed, experiencing brief vertigo as she turned to maneuver on the top rung. She managed to clamber down and drop quietly into the grass next to Cato.

They stood at the front of the barn facing the house. Yelling voices reached them now, as well as another pattering of gunfire, and Cato put a finger to his lips and nodded in the direction of dark forms ambling in the direction of the homestead. None of them had spotted Nina and her big friend...yet.

"We gonna have to go around. We can't—"

"Follow me," Cato said, then, "Wait. Hold on." He reached inside the open barn door and retrieved a long shaft, and Nina noticed it had a curved hook coming off the side and a spike at the end. It looked more like some durn gothic weapon than a logging tool. "This'll do. Got me a peavey hook."

A bullet bit into the barn, chipping off a piece of wood. Cato ducked, wide-eyed. "Good Heavens! All right, let's get," he hissed as he hunched over and angled toward the back of the homestead, clutching his new weapon.

Nina kept to the man's heels. It was a quiet, deadly run. Any deaduns they came across they dispatched quickly and quietly, her with her knife and Cato with his spear-hook thing. The biters never even seen 'em til it was too late. Soon they had made it around the back of the homestead, panting and hunkered down behind a row of bushes against the stone foundation.

Nina climbed up and over the railing and set foot on the porch, Cato right behind her. They tried to be stealthy about it, but the old wood creaked and groaned under the big man's weight, some of the boards warping beneath his booted feet.

"Everyone's in a panic," he whispered. "How we do this without getting ourselves shot? They might mistake us for one of those things."

As if reinforcing the statement, another spattering of gunfire rang out from the front of the house. Cato about jumped out of his half-clothed skin, and Nina drew her Colt Navy, glad she'd spared the ammunition. It fit snug in her hand despite her blistered palm.

"Can you whistle?" she asked.

Cato smiled, his teeth flashing in the dark. "I know more tunes than I can count. Some I done made up myself. You should hear me play 'Ol' Dan Tucker' on the five-string. Lord, I miss my *bangie*."

Nina patted his bare arm. "I hope I get to. For now you just whistle one of them tunes. I'll lead the way."

And he did. A lilting, Irish-sounding melody sounded from his lips, lifting into the foul air with the brightness of a sunrise. Nina started off, rounded the north corner of the homestead, and ran smack into the solid shadow of someone coming round the other side.

CHAPTER TEN

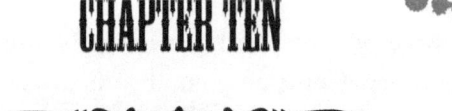

GEORGE WAS A LITTLE slow on the draw. His rifle came up a full second after Nina's blade touched his unshaven throat. She smiled upon seeing him and sheathed her knife, then frowned. His head was leaking blood again.

George cursed at nearly getting his throat cut, but nodded when he recognized Nina. "Thought you was a goner."

"What happened to your head?"

George shook it. "My head?"

"You're bleedin."

He rubbed his hand across his head and looked at his fingers. "Shit. I scrapped with more than one of those

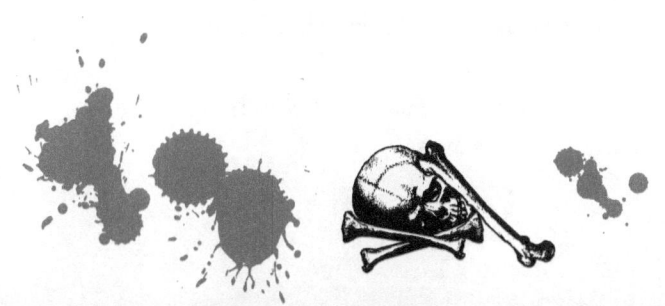

deaduns. Who knows? Now you mention it, same fuckin' spot I hit it on before…throbs like the dickens. Not sure what it is about my head these days…"

"You mean it bein' so empty and all?"

George sneered. "Fuck you, squaw."

"And fuck you sideways, you scaly-assed Confederate *fucknut*."

George put his hands on his hips, then snickered. "Alright then. Come on around. Whoa, damn!" His gaze alighted on Cato. "Didn't even see you there, ni…I mean… uh, where's yer shirt?"

"Them deaduns tore it right offa me."

George nodded. "All right, well, come on." He walked off, waving Nina and Cato to follow. "Don't shoot," he said as he rounded the corner of the house, followed by, "Look who's back from the dead."

A shadow hurried toward her, grasped her shoulders, and squeezed her. "I thought I lost ya, girl."

Nina squeezed back, and she meant it. "I'm fine, Pa."

"I'm serious, Nina. Don't ever do that again…" Then he hugged her hard a second time.

"Couldn't be helped. Got penned in, but I was with Cato here. I owe him."

"No, ma'am," Cato said. "I wouldn't be here now if it weren't for you."

Before the big man finished his sentence James Manning crushed her in a hug of his own. "Christ, Nina. You scared the living hell out of us. Don't know what I would have done if…"

"You woulda went on," she said, but she thought she saw moisture in the man's eyes.

Buck stepped back from the porch rail, interrupting the moment. "Gotta reload, James. Need ya, son. Glad you're still with us, Nina." The roughrider sat down at a table illuminated with a partially-shuttered lantern. Pouches of powder and lead balls were scattered across the surface. Buck began assembling loads for his pistol.

Manning nodded and gave Nina a peck on the forehead, then hurried to the porch rail. He aimed a dragoon into the yard and ripped off a shot.

Nina grabbed George's lantern from him and shined it about. Mason, Mathias, and Red Thunder were at the rail dealing with the gathering crowd of deaduns around the homestead, George going to join them. Pa sat down across from Buck and worked on his own loads.

Where were the girls?

Then she saw them hunched against the wall between two rocking chairs. Jasmine was slumped over, her head in Rachel's arms. "Nina, thank the Lord," the black woman said, reaching up. "Thought you were dead."

Nina knelt and took Jasmine's blood-covered fingers in her own. "I'm fine. What happened?"

Jasmine lightly touched the back of her neck, winced. "Just a scratch. Biter caught up to me...didn't even see it in all the mess. Got me as I fought the bastards. Couldn't get away. But you never guess who saved me."

Nina raised her brows.

"Goddamn George Daggett. Now I owe him."

"You don't owe either of those Daggetts nothing but a boot up the backside. Speaking of, where's Strobridge?"

"Mister Ramdohr sent one of his men with Strobridge to fetch a wagon. Him and Greta and another man are gathering supplies."

"Good," said Nina. "Guess Ramdohr understands we need to head for the hills."

Rachel chimed in, "He said they ain't coming."

"What? That don't make no sense."

"He don't seem a very reasonable man," Rachel responded, still clinging tight to Jasmine.

Some strands of hair were pasted to Rachel's cheek and Nina brushed them away, then shook her head as she looked at Jasmine. "Imagine that. An unreasonable man."

Both of them smiled.

"You gonna be okay, Jaz?"

The woman nodded and gripped Nina's hand. "I'm fine, girl. Just tired of runnin'..."

"You rest." Nina gave Jasmine's hand a squeeze, then she went and squatted by Pa as he loaded. The scent of stale beer wafted off him. She was sure her father regretted drinkin' tonight. They probably *all* did. In the space of a few minutes, they'd almost cashed in. Likely because they'd been too stupid drunk to move their asses with any degree of urgency. But she wouldn't let herself regret what happened between her and James tonight. No, not one bit, and she'd do it again if given the chance.

"What's the outlook?"

Pa's face was sweaty, his lip quivering as he measured powder into the cylinder. "It's grim, darlin', but we're holdin' 'em for now."

"Not for long," she said, miserable to be the bearer of such bad tidings. "Cato and I climbed up on the roof back at the barn. There's gotta be a thousand of them coming out of them woods."

Pa nodded, took a deep breath. He took her hand, and she could tell his was shaking. "Mister Ramdohr offered to get us a wagon, take us to safety."

"That's what I hea—"

The front door burst open and Nina took a hop back and got to her feet. Ramdohr's pit bulldogs came tearing out, huffing and puffing and straining at the ends of their long chains. At the other end was Jon Ramdohr, chains wrapped around one arm, his cane in the other. "Intruders," he spat, his face quivering and eyes glaring. "Damn yard's full of intruders!"

"Before long they will be everywhere," Father Mathias said, stepping into the dim halo of lantern light. He looked a haggard sight in those bleak, flickering shadows. "Hundreds, maybe a thousand. Do you understand what we're dealing with here, Mister Ramdohr?"

Ramdohr scowled and glared out into the yard. "I see ruffians...an army of lawless *anfallare*..." He adjusted his scowl to the shooters standing against the porch rail. "...and a bunch of fools who can't shoot worth a damn."

George Daggett pulled the trigger on his pistol. A shadow dropped in the yard. He turned to look at Ramdohr. "How you like that piece of shootin', Mister Big Britches?"

"We're scoring hits, Mister Ramdohr," Father Mathias interrupted George. The priest stepped as near as he dared to the man, staying just out of reach of those worked-up hounds. "But as a man of God, you must believe me when I say raiders they may be, but these are no ruffians."

Ramdohr stiffened, his face visibly reddening even in the dimness of the porch. Nina thought he might release his hounds on Mathias for a second. "You come to my house under the guise of peace and a mean crew of interlopers come trailing after you! I've a mind to hand you over to them."

"Just keep those coonhounds bawling and they'll take care of that for ya," George tossed back.

"I think the guns might be attracting them more than the hounds," Buck ventured as he stood and returned to the porch rail, relieving Manning. Deaduns were coming in numbers now. Buck was correct. The incessant sounds of gunfire was most assuredly drawing them in. Some biters were feeling their way around the stone foundation. Red Thunder patrolled the porch, braining them with his tomahawk.

"Getting low on ammo here," Mason called out. "Where's the damn wagon at?"

Ramdohr squinted, pointed the tip of his cane at Mathias. "The only reason I allowed any of you here was because of your association with Mister Strobridge. I've seen ruffians before, and I'll not have any man, even a man of the Lord, tell me what kind of interlopers are on my property."

"Mister Ramdohr, please," Mathias replied, "retire within your home until—"

"Look, you deuced idiot," George came off the rail. "They're living dead. Corpses sprung to life just like...like evil bloomin' flowers or some strange shit."

"You keep your mouth shut before I sic these hounds on you. I don't abide deceivers or troublemakers, and I've already heard enough out of you." The sawmill boss turned to Cato. "Where's Christopher and Miguel? I need you three to deal with this situation, since Mister Strobridge's men obviously cannot handle matters."

Cato cowered before his angry boss. "I'm sorry, Mister Ramdohr, but Chris and Miguel, they's dead."

"What?" Ramdohr's jaw dropped. He started to bluster just as his daughter threw open the door. The dogs yanked at their chains and growled.

Greta had her ax in hand, while right behind her came one of Ramdohr's other log men with a shotgun. The big girl nodded at Father Mathias. "We put some airtights and water on the back porch. Ready for y'all to take 'em." She wrinkled her nose. "Oh, what's that god-awful stench?"

Mathias skirted Ramdohr's hounds and placed his hand on Greta's shoulder. "That would be the walking dead, my dear. Hell has descended upon the world, and now it visits your homestead. I beg you and yours to gather what you can and accompany us. There is nothing here anymore but death."

Greta glanced about uncertainly, then peered out into the yard where the complaints of deaduns grew louder by the minute. "I do what my...what...what *are* they?" Greta stuttered. It was clear she just made out the situation a lot more plainly than her mule-ass of a father.

"I'm out," Mason announced. He tucked his pistol in his belt and loosed his knife.

"Same here," said Buck. He hefted an ax and went about helping Red Thunder clear deaduns from the rail.

Jon Ramdohr fumed. "I'll show you how to run interlopers off your property. *Fan dårar!* The only tolerable one among you is Mister Strobridge..."

Nina almost chuckled at that, despite the goings-on,

suddenly not so sure this crusty old Ramdohr feller was much count at that point, considering his lofty estimation of the self-interested railroad boss. What she didn't expect was for him to march to the edge of the porch with his dogs, scattering the Daggetts out of his way, and calling his man to follow. "Greta, stay! Gustaf!"

"Ja?"

"Let's show these *inkompetent idioter* the meaning of *Sisu!*"

"Ja!" Gustaf went down the porch steps behind his boss, albeit somewhat hesitantly.

"Sic 'em!" Ramdohr hollered, turning loose of his hounds.

Nina went to the porch rail, opening the lantern to shed enough light for the fools to see by—to give them *some* kind of chance.

The massive hounds charged in amongst the deadun ranks, grasping rotted arms and legs, pulling biters off balance, shaking them like toys. One dog flew back with a deadun hand in its mouth. The growling beast dropped it and went in for more.

No, Nina thought, but it was too late. For all their ferociousness, the dogs didn't stand a chance. Deaduns were immune to pain, and they simply fell on the poor animals and started tearing them to pieces. The barks turned into yelps and howls.

"*Gå av, era djävlar!* Get off my dogs!" Ramdohr lifted his cane and charged into the mass ripping away at his hounds. His man, Gustaf, yelled out for him, but went charged in his wake regardless, blasting a deadun before several came up and grabbed his arms, pulling him screaming to the ground.

"*Far!*" Greta tromped down the steps and into the yard, chasing after her father. She caught up with the sawmill owner just as he broke his cane over a deadun's head. The big girl took one of her father's arms, but a deadun got hold of the other. A third biter fell on Ramdohr and sunk its teeth into his shoulder.

The man screamed. Greta cried out, pulling even harder, so strong she nearly got her father free. But more deaduns grabbed hold and clung like they always did once they had you. Fingers clenched like vices, arms with steel-banded strength driven by evil, mouths clamping on flesh, chewing, tearing.

Jon Ramdohr came apart at the shoulder with a bloody *pop*, leaving Greta holding his arm, red tendons hanging from the stump. The rest of him disappeared screaming into the mass of hungry monsters.

Nina aimed her pistol at the hellish mob. "Greta!" she called, not willing to abandon the girl if she could get her wits about her. "Come on! He's gone."

Greta hung on to her father's arm, her blubbering sobs somehow competing with the moaning mass of deaduns. With an angry scream, she swung the arm at the nearest deadun, catching it in the face and sending it sprawling. She swung it again in a backhanded stroke and knocked another across the gob where it went ass-over-elbows to the ground. It didn't put either of 'em down for good, but it was nonetheless impressive. She wanted to fight on, but the deaduns were closing, and she found herself surrounded by the same reaching, red-stained hands that had just ripped Jon Ramdohr to pieces.

Greta threw her father's arm down, hitched up her skirts, and rushed back toward the house, deaduns loping, hissing after her. She ascended the stairs as Red Thunder and Buck hacked away at her pursuers. At the top, she looked with horrified eyes at Nina. "You were right," she panted, her face splattered with gore. "They're as dead as anything I ever saw that was dead. But…*how?*"

"It's a long story."

"It's that fuckin' bayou magic," George shouted. "What they call it?"

"Voodoo?" Mason answered.

"That's it. Walking dead, devils, evil spirits and shit…" George paused to put a bullet in a deadun trying to reach through the railing. "The end of the fuckin' world."

Nina pulled Greta away. "Never mind them. They're just tryin' to scare you is all—"

Mason was suddenly in Nina's face. "You don't know shit, you know that?"

Nina's first instinct was to fetch him another rap in the nose just like she done a couple days ago, but something calmed within her. Something about Mason's eyes. Fear? Uncertainty? He suddenly seemed just a scared boy in all this hellabaloo.

And then, in a surprising move, he stepped around Nina and put his hand on Greta's back, bringing the girl into his embrace. She folded into Mason, sobs shaking her. "*Min far,*" she said in what must be her native tongue, Nina reckoned. "*Min far…*"

"They're all comin'," George yelled. "All of 'em!"

"Here." Mason pushed Greta into Nina's arms, and the woman laid her head on Nina's shoulder, still sobbing at the sudden grisly loss of her father. The men formed a line at the top of the porch steps: Manning, Mason, George, and Cato, side-by-side with their guns and blades, while her pa, Red Thunder, and Buck went from spot-to-spot to keep the deaduns from pulling the rails apart.

Nina awkwardly patted Greta's back a couple times. "Hey, mourn later." She held the woman at arm's length, looking up into her watery eyes—she had to be a good six inches taller. Nina bent and picked up Greta's ax, so dumbstruck was she that she'd rushed to her father's rescue without it. Nina pushed it into her hands. "They come at you, use it, hear me?"

Greta nodded, sniffling. She wiped her eyes on her sleeve and nodded again.

Then Jasmine and Rachel started screaming.

A PACK OF DEADUNS FILED around the corner of the house. "Deaduns *on the porch!*" Nina yelled. They'd somehow figured out a way up around the side or back and made their way to the front, likely drawn to the ruckus.

Rachel screamed again and the leader, a deadun with a large gouge out of its cheek, extended its arms and shuffled for her. She was still huddled with Jasmine against the wall, and it snatched at her skirts, baring its teeth. Rachel kicked and extended her legs to keep it away, but it was a pertinacious cuss.

Jasmine leaned across Rachel, started pushing at the deadun's head, her hand perilously close to its gnashing teeth. A second one came to pile on, but Red Thunder intercepted it, burying his tomahawk in the back of its skull. He whipped around to help the women but two more grabbed him and he was forced to fight them off.

Damn! There was at least ten of 'em and still more rounding that corner of the porch, coming single file, as if getting themselves into a doggone Sunday gospel mill—but they was fixin' to prey in a different manner than the churchy meaning of the word.

Nina rushed forward as the deadun setting on the girls grabbed Jasmine's arm in both its hand and drew its lips back. Jasmine screamed and tugged to no avail. That mouth opened wide, maggots spilling out, then Nina pulled the trigger on her iron and put a load point blank in the bastard's piehole. The back of its head decorated the wall and the deadun sagged sidewise like a big sack of rotten apples.

Nina went to help Rachel and Jasmine to their feet, saying, "We gotta get inside!"

Then she saw one grab Pa from behind and she leapt on the damn thing, grabbed the back of its ratty coat and yanked, slinging the deadun to the floorboards. It rolled into the back of Red Thunder's legs and nearly tripped the Indian up, but he managed to recover and swipe his weapon down on its crown as it struggled to get up.

Pa turned. "Look out!" he yelled, pointing behind her. Nina ducked sideways, narrowly avoiding a pair of swiping arms.

Manning was there and put a bullet in its temple. "We're done here," he hollered. "Through the house!" He pointed his dragoon at another and put it down, but it was replaced by two more.

Buck yelled, "Let's get the hell out of here!" He flung

the front door open and started to push Greta through; she'd been standing paralyzed the whole time. "Come on!"

Father Mathias stood in between Buck and the Daggetts, peering about and looking more weary than panic-struck. The brothers were falling back, measured, shoulder to shoulder, Mason stabbing his knife in and out, George using his rifle's stock to whack deaduns to the left and right. The defense had thinned on the porch steps so the horde was invading from that direction now, as well.

"Get inside, goddammit!" George bawled. "Jesus!"

Red screamed a war cry that made Nina's hair stand on end. She looked to see him and Cato like two warriors of olden times, the Indian swinging his tomahawk and holding a knife in a reverse grip in the other, spinning and stabbing, while the big man lanced deaduns through their heads with the spike on the end of his hooked spear and kicked them away. It was a wall of biters and the two men were reaping a bloody harvest. Even so, some flopped by their vicious attacks, while others lurched up the porch steps. They were overrun.

Suddenly Rachel lifted one of the oil lamps and before Nina could yell stop she smashed it over a deadun reaching for Jasmine. Gouts of liquid fire splashed, lighting it up, though it didn't deviate from its target, its fiery arms grasping wildly.

Jasmine dodged away from it and within arm's reach of Buck, who readily seized hold of her arm and catapulted the woman through the open door and into the house. "Let's bail out! Everyone! Red! Cato!" Buck yelled.

Nina fired her last shot at a deadun coming up the steps.

"Let's go!" Pa yanked her by the elbow, and she turned

to see the one that was on fire was bumping into others, and within the blink of an eye, two more of 'em became walking torches.

Buck pushed Rachel through the doorway next, then ushered Father Mathias inside. Manning buffeted a tooth-clacking female deadun with the butt of one of his dragoons as he came up against Nina and Pa. "Go," he said, kicked another in the chest, knocking it backwards into more of 'em. "Go, go, go!" he yelled again and shoved them toward the door.

"Mason, George, come on!"

"Trying!" George was struggling to disencumber himself from a biter that had taken hold of his shirt. Cato was there of a sudden. He used the hook part of his spear to chop the deadun's arm off at the elbow. The black man and the Confederate looked at one another for all of half-a-second, and George nodded his thanks.

"Red!" Buck yelled as Nina, Pa, and the Daggetts rushed inside. Mason ducked beneath an attempted fiery deadun-hug before he ran in and promptly stumbled over a bunched-up rug. He hit the floor and cussed as he got back up, Pa helping with a hand beneath Mason's arm.

Manning, Cato, Buck, and Red Thunder hurried inside, in that order, with James careening into Nina but holding her steady. Red tried to pull the door shut, but a burning biter wedged itself in, the heat forcing the Indian back.

"Go!" someone yelled—multiple someones, in fact, and the entire group dashed down the wood-paneled hallway as biting, blazing deaduns infested the entry.

"This way!" Greta hollered from the front, leading them toward the back of the house. Buck tossed a hall table in the deaduns' path, then he and Red overturned a bureau to further halt their progress. Rugs and drapes were starting to alight, and the stench of roasting-hot flesh and sinew seared Nina's nostrils.

Jasmine was having trouble, so Nina and Rachel put her between them and helped her along. Nina caught flashes of family portraits, old, washed-out photographs with frowning people in them—one in particular struck her, a daguerreotype of a younger Jonathan Ramdohr in a dark coat and necktie, a well-dressed girl and a dapper little boy in his lap, one to each knee, and a light-haired woman in a fine dress standing next to them. The woman, who she reckoned to be Greta's ma, had a wistful, far-off aspect. For reasons unknown even to herself, Nina took it off the wall and tucked it beneath her arm.

Red Thunder put down a flaming deadun behind them as the rest made haste into the large kitchen. As if on cue, Strobridge flung open the back door. He looked at the haggard group and the fire-clothed deaduns behind them and smiled his shitty grin. "Wagon's loaded and leaving the station, and none too soon by the looks of it. *Whoo— whooo!*"

"Lead the way," Manning said, having no patience for the boss man.

Unlike the hallway, the kitchen still smelled like boiled cabbage and potatoes, and a cherry pie sat cooling in the center of the table. Strobridge had been eating well, it seemed.

They poured out onto the back porch, and Nina saw the wagon. It looked like a boat, wide and long with tall sides and an expansive, covered top. It had been pulled alongside the house, the tail thrown open. Greta grabbed up a small box of goods from the porch and went down the back steps, tossing it in the wagon.

"Forget loadin' up!" George said. "Let's go."

Greta lowered her brow at him. "Daddy brought that from Pennsylvania, called it his Conestoga Lady." And indeed, *Conestoga Lady* was painted across its side in bold, golden letters.

Nina and Rachel assisted Jasmine into the back of the wagon while Cato, still bare-chested, and Father Mathias, grabbed a couple more crates and conveyed them to the back of the wagon. Rachel climbed up and pulled the crates inside, while George and Mason stood there panting, covered in bloodstains and soot and combing the surrounds with their eyes. Manning stood guard, as well, while Buck and Red Thunder were evidently still in the kitchen creating more obstructions with the furnishings judging from the racket.

Pa clutched Nina's arm. "Nina, I don't think I can…."

She saw his face alight in the lantern's glow. He was losing it. His eyes had a blank look about them. His hands shook. "Take it easy, Pa. Just climb in."

"No, Nina. You don't understand. I'm tired…*damn* tired. And what you talked about the other day in the fort about your ma. I believe she's watching over us. I believe she wants me to come to her. I think you all should leave me behind…" he peered upward. "Let me lay in yonder patch of wild thyme and look up at that beautiful full moon through the trees."

Nina grabbed Pa by his coat collar with one hand and slapped him across the face with the other, and none too lightly. "Don't you do this! Don't you tell me what I see! Or make your own goddamn accounts of *my* dreams. Mine! Truth be told, throughout this whole world-gone-mad shitstorm, I ain't heard a damn peep from Ma. She ain't appeared, she ain't whispered, she ain't even banged a fuckin' drum..."

Pa held his hand to his cheek. "What?"

Nina shook her head. "Pa, you givin' up ain't gonna happen. I know you're tired. I know you think we're doomed—and maybe we are—but you ain't givin' up on me. On *us*. I will throw your butt up into this wagon, and George can laugh his ass off while I do it. You want that?"

Indeed, she was quite aware that George and Mason had both stopped looking around and were watching this little drama play out. "Hell, I'll help toss him up in there," said Mason.

The old man smiled weakly, glanced over at the Daggetts, then back at Nina. "No," he said, his voice soft with calm. Then said it again, real low. It reminded Nina of how Clara Buell had sounded once she'd resolved to die. But at least he was cooperating.

"We need to scoot," Mason said as Cato came up and put another crate in the wagon.

The big man nodded. "That'd be it."

The horses up front were shifting in their traces, plainly disquieted by deaduns wandering toward the wagon from other parts of the yard. At the same time, Buck and Red came out the back door, blood on top of blood, looking like they'd been at the butcher block.

"All right! Let's go," Manning called out, and for the first time Nina noticed a man standing in the driver's seat.

"Where's Mister Ramdohr?" the man asked.

"He's dead," George said. "Now take hold of them reins and let's vamoose."

The man leveled his shotgun at them.

"You gotta be jokin'. Look around, shithead."

Greta edged George aside and fixed the man a stern look. "Rory, Daddy's dead, and there's things coming I can't explain that want to do us harm. You see them coming upon us now. Look around. There's about a hundred—"

"More like a thousand," Nina added.

"—a *thousand* coming from the north. A whole mob is in the house right now, Rory."

The driver looked rattled. He shifted position, steadying himself on the seat. "You come up, Greta. You too, Mister Strobridge."

Manning put his hands on his hips. "Look, time's running out. So, like George said, either get us going or I'll pull you down myself and leave your ass here. Make your choice, because we're *leaving*."

Rory growled and aimed his barrel at Manning. "No. Greta, you climb up. *We're* leaving. I swore to your daddy to take care of you, and that didn't include nobody else. Now, you and Mister Strobridge, come on! The rest of you—"

"You're making a mistake." Manning got that hard look in his eyes, the same one he'd gotten with Woodie before he beat the living hell out of him.

"You might want to listen to him," Strobridge advised. "Or shoot now."

Nina pulled her knife loose. "You shoot him, I'll kill you."

A pair of deaduns drew within ten yards, catching Nina's attention, but Cato hefted his hook-spear, and trotted toward them. "I got this. Just don't leave me."

Nina nodded, turned back to the situation, just as the horses spooked hard and the reins were pulled from Rory's hand. He bent to retrieve them, and that's when the Daggetts were on him.

Quick as a snake, Mason grabbed the barrel and yanked the shotgun away. Strobridge leaned back as George pulled Rory down off the seat. The man slipped as he came down, landing stomach first on the rail, his breath leaving his lungs in a violent *whoosh*.

Buck was there, grabbing Rory up by the back of his trousers and tossing him onto the porch. George ran up after him and kicked the man twice in the ribs.

"Stop it!" Greta yelled. Rachel was leaning out the back of the wagon, yelling "please stop!" and Mathias was shaking his head, murmuring, "Good Lord."

Manning grabbed George's arm before he could land a third kick. "Let him be. Let's just go."

George laughed. "Ye're a stupid bastard, Manning. Idiot was gonna blow your brains out."

"No need for him to die. He was just protecting—" Manning clutched his stomach and removed Rory's knife from it, the man on his knees trying to drive the blade back in.

Nina gasped at seeing blood color James Manning's shirt, a deeper black against the gore already there. Her heart thumped inside her throat.

Manning twisted the knife out of Rory's hand, eliciting a yelp from the man. He threw it down, pulled one of his dragoons from his hip, and blew a half-dollar sized hole through Rory's chest. The man pitched backward, dead as a door nail.

Nina ran to James, putting her hand over his stomach, felt warm, wet blood. She glanced at the dead driver, his sightless blue eyes staring at her.

And then a familiar shriek came from the sky.

C ATO STOOD AMIDST A pile of deaduns, looking up into the dark sky, while Nina wondered how long it would be before all of Liao Xu's minions arrived.

"One of those flying things again!" the big man hollered, jogging back to the wagon. "My God, you all killed Rory?"

"The man wouldn't listen to reason," Strobridge said, up on the driver's bench seat, his eyes roving the sky. "What was that infernal howling noise?"

"Get me to the wagon," Manning told Nina, and he leaned on her. Pa and Buck helped him up and they all piled in on top of the crates, all except for Greta Ramdohr, who leaned over Rory on the porch and put her hand over the hole in his chest.

Suddenly arms crashed through the Ramdohr's back door, splintering wood, and tearing the frame to pieces. A mass of crispy deaduns belched forth. Greta fell back on her ass, narrowly missed by the tumbling corpses. One of them snatched at Rory's still-warm body and fell upon it, biting as it burned.

Mason hopped out of the wagon bed as Greta screamed. A smoldering deadun crawled at her, but Mason sprinted up the steps and kicked it away. "Come on!" he yelled, swiping a few licks of flame off his trousers. He offered his hand.

Greta snatched up her ax and took Mason's hand, and together they ran to the front of the wagon while more biters and long, hungry curlicues of flickering fire continued to pour out of the Ramdohr homestead. George and Strobridge made room for Mason and Greta in the front, and with a *ya-yah-giddyap* the wagon lurched and began trundling off down the dirt lane.

A smoking deadun caught up to them and grabbed the back of the wagon, but Cato used his long weapon to push it away. The biter was a weakened, blackened mess, so it just fell and laid there reaching for them, working its jaws and gurgling.

Manning rested between Nina's legs, his head on her chest. She kept her hand over the wound but it wouldn't quit bleeding. Buck tossed her his shirt, which he'd never been able to get on. She thanked him and held the cloth against the spot. Nina was skeptical about having tears left to cry, but they came.

Nina glanced over to find Rachel Buell sitting beside her on a crate, watching as she worried over Manning. The girl had a blank look on her face, but something in there was trying to get out, trying to make sense of all this shit.

"I miss my ma," Rachel said flatly, and laid her head on Jasmine's shoulder as moans of frustration—or at least Nina imagined it so—hounded them until the wagon turned a bend and the burning homestead crawling with deaduns faded from view.

CHAPTER ELEVEN

Hot anger welled up in Nina's brain. She could have done more back there at the mill. All she felt like she'd done was stand around on that porch while the men did most of the fighting. Hell, Mason had shoved tearful Greta Ramdohr into Nina's arms as if she were some damn Mama Hen or something.

And then she let poor James get stabbed!

She peered at the top of Father Mathias' dark-haired head as he bent over James Manning. The priest had one hand on James' stomach, the other clutching his beaded rosary. Mathias' lips moved in silent prayer, and James, in his somewhat senseless state, moved his head to the side and grimaced.

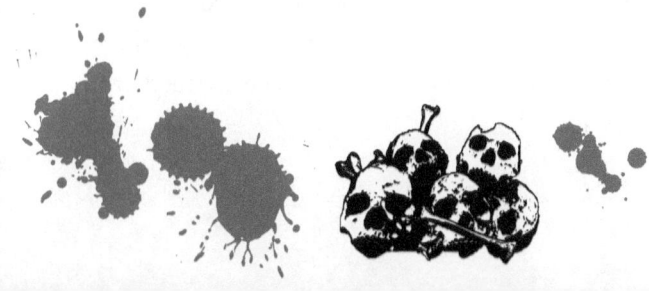

James was drenched in sweat, and his color had not looked good before, but it seemed to be returning a little as Mathias dispensed his priestly healing. Nina wiped his clammy brow and wondered if the man she was falling for was going to die this very night.

"That should hold him a while," Father Mathias said, putting his rosary away. "The blood flow has slowed significantly, but unfortunately it's all I can do. I'm sorry."

"Is he gonna die?"

"He is a strong man, very grounded in this world…" Mathias was in the process of scooting back when the wagon bounced over a rut or a rock causing the priest to plunk right into Buck.

The roughrider grabbed Mathias' shoulder and helped him sit up straight. "You okay, Father?"

"I'm fine, my friend. Thank you." But he didn't look fine, even in the dim light beneath the wagon cover.

Rachel offered him a canteen. Mathias thanked her and took a modest swallow, then gave it back. Rachel turned to Nina. "Here, Nina."

Nina didn't want a blasted drink, was perfectly fine feeling pitiful and sore. But one look into Rachel's well-meaning eyes and she relented, took a long draw, thanked the girl, and went to hand the canteen back.

"What about Mister Manning?" Rachel had taken it upon herself to ensure everyone got some water. It was her way of doing something, *anything*, to keep her mind occupied—proving her worth, as it were, if only to herself, Nina reckoned. The girl had even crawled through the front flap to water the drivers, men she'd been terrified of just a few days ago.

Nina put the metal lip of the canteen on James' lips and slowly tipped it up. Even just a capful would be helpful. Most the water dribbled out the side of his mouth, though. Hopefully he'd get some of it down.

She lifted the shirt away, taking off the pressure she'd been putting on the stab wound, and checked it. The priest had done good work. It seeped, but was no longer leaking like it was ten minutes ago.

"Sorry about your shirt, Buck," she said. It was saturated with Manning's blood.

"Least somebody got some use out of it." The roughrider was still bare-chested, as was Cato, who sat by Greta at the back of the wagon.

Strobridge could be heard jawing up front, mostly to himself. Nina half expected one of the Daggetts to put a bullet in the man just to shut his hole—but then, they were almost out of bullets. Even so, the boss man seemed to be the only one in a talky mood. Nina did her best to ignore the man's unrelenting palaver.

She gazed at Greta, who stared out behind them in slack disbelief, likely thinking of how her entire life had just pretty much been throttled to death. Cato sat beside her, displaying the same stupefied gape. Nina reckoned they both had the selfsame expression that'd been on her mug not so long ago. A big blank stare, her mind trying to work out how dead folks were up and ambling about, attacking the living on sight, and later pondering what was left of the person inside. It was hard enough dealing with death...*but undeath?*

Pa occupied a spot in the corner atop a thin blanket, curled up like an old dog. He'd passed out before they'd hit the south road to Carson City. Good. He needed it. They all did, but Nina hoped a little shuteye would help bring back some of her father's fire.

Red Thunder slept as well, leaning against the front wall of the wagon, just beneath the flap. Even a great warrior needed sleep now and again. Red had woken only long enough to give Rachel use of his shoulder as a stepping stool while she offered water to the drivers.

Nina looked down at Jasmine, passed out on the floor next to Manning. The woman's face twitched, her hands jerking as she worked out whatever nightmare had come to cloud her troubled sleep. The wound on her neck, now cleaned and blessed by Father Mathias, wasn't as messy, but there was a swelling beneath the scar, the bruise boldly showing in the dim moonlight on her dark skin. Even that much was a miracle, though.

Finally, she peered across at Father Mathias. He sat with his elbows on his knees, and his face in his hands. He seemed small, his good humor beaten down to a fraction of its former self.

"Why don't you sleep, Father?"

Mathias drew his hands down across his face, gave Nina a wan smile. "The same reason you don't. You're racking your brain to understand all this, to think of a way to beat Liao Xu, to save the people you love; yet, you're too tired to think, too tired to work it all out…"

Nina sighed, weariness making it easy to agree, even if his explanation was far from the truth. "That about sums it up, I guess." Her voice sounded rough, tired, like claws had raked her throat on the inside. "I do have a question."

"Go on."

"What is *alignalghi?*"

Mathias steepled his hands in front of his lips for a moment, then said, "It means 'he or she who knows.' It is an ancient word for one who can travel between the world of the fleshly body and that of the spirits."

"Like a shaman."

"Of a kind, yes. But there is much to it, and I know just enough to likely lead you astray rather than be of actual service."

Nina furrowed her brow. *Then why the hell bring it up?* "Do you know anyone else who…"

"Liao."

She scoffed. "Sure. I'll just waltz up to the sonofabitch and ask him to share some of his 'heavenly' mysteries before I put a bullet in his ass."

"It will take much more than getting shot in the backside to stop—"

"I know, I know. So how *are* we going to stop him?"

"I'm still trying to understand how he caught back up so quickly. Pursuing the rails was a logical course, but knowing we'd travel across the wilderness and then point his undead to the very location of our respite… They couldn't have found us unless Liao sent them ahead, almost as if he was sure of our direction."

"Maybe he just scattered the deaduns from Reno in every direction and got lucky."

"I suppose." His voice lowered, eyes narrowing. "But is it too farfetched to suggest someone is dropping crumbs?"

The thought had never occurred. Nina was skeptical. Someone among their own guiding Liao Xu to them? That was wild charge, yet… "*Who?*"

Mathias's eyes widened, glanced to the front of the wagon. He didn't have to say it. She knew he meant Strobridge, and it wouldn't surprise Nina in the least.

"How can we know for sure?"

Mathias held out his hands and shrugged. "The knowledge escapes me. I can only believe the Lord will reveal the answer to me at some point. When? I don't know."

Nina tried not to sound angry, but this conversation was maddening. "Blind faith? How can you live like that? Hoping for the best, for some damn *miracle all the time.*"

"Therein lies the adventure, my dear."

"Horseshit."

Mathias tilted his head. "Horseshit? Are you not responsible for a few miracles yourself over the last couple of days? Or would you say that was just pulling it out your ass?"

Nina frowned. "It ain't something I *wanted.*" She looked away before Mathias could see the guilt in her eyes. "To be honest, I asked the *boha gande* to take me with him. I wanted to stay in the spirit world. I would have abandoned my father...James too. Truth be told, Father, I'm a coward."

Mathias pursed his lips, then took a breath, but before he could speak a deep cough drew their attention. Cato had turned to face them, the whites of his eyes standing out in the moonlight. "You sayin' there's someone behind all this?"

"Unfortunately, there is. Someone bent on turning the world we know into a hellish place of bedlam and turmoil, where the dead rise and do his bidding."

Cato nodded, gulped so dry Nina could hear it from where she sat. "The end of the world?"

"I fear so, yes."

Rachel raised her head. "My mom got tore in half," she said, informing the big man, saying it as if she were relating what happened in school that day. Nina wondered how much she'd heard of the exchange with Father Mathias.

Cato winced; the man wore others' pain well. "Your mama? Teared in two?"

"Yep. Back at the fort."

"Where we holed up before," Nina explained.

"This man is some kinda monster?"

"Of a sort," Mathias said. "But you're on the right side. Or, the side of right, I should say. Are you feeling up to the Lord's task?"

Cato's posture went stiff and uncertain. "Don't seem like I have much choice."

Mathias nodded. "The Lord has a way of putting us in impossible situations to put us to the test." He pulled out his Bible and began thumbing through the pages.

Suddenly George Daggett pushed aside the wagon flap. "Any of that beer in those supplies?"

The wagon swayed a moment, then Greta, who was leaning against Cato's bare back, spoke up. "No beer. No whiskey." Her voice was a forlorn sounding croak, obviously dried up from having shed a barrelful of tears.

"Fuckin' figures." The flap dropped with a ruffle.

Nina shifted, trying to be easy; Manning's unconscious weight had numbed her legs some time ago. She found a more comfortable position and let the creaking, rocking motion of the wagon send her into a bit of a fog. She trusted they were going somewhere, and put it out of her head that Strobridge could be taking them to Liao Xu. The railroad boss was a bastard and a half, but it just plumb didn't make much sense.

She leaned back and reflected. They'd gotten out of another mess, but not without injury. Nina flexed her right hand. Stiff, swollen, blistered. Not much of her wasn't. She took the canteen from Rachel's lap, poured a little water on her hands, and wiped them uselessly, on her shirt.

They hadn't even gotten more than an hour's rest, and what had they cost Liao? *Nothing*. He seemed to have a ready supply of rotting flesh at his beckoning. Nina had no ideas about how they should proceed. She reckoned she should feel lucky—her pa and Manning were alive, at least for now, but James might not stay that way unless proper care could be found. She didn't know a durn thing about this Carson City, either. In any case, Nina wasn't getting nowhere just going round and round in her head. "You know," she said in low whisper, then cleared her dry throat. "When Jasmine wakes up, we'll have to see if she feels like singing. You should hear her," she said that last bit to Cato.

The big man smiled and looked over at the sleeping woman. "I bet she has a beautiful singing voice."

Rachel looked at her, too. "Should I wake her?"

"No," Nina hissed, a bit harsh. Seeing Rachel's hurt expression, she said, "Sorry, I'm just feelin' sour."

Rachel's face brightened. "*I* can sing."

"I'd love to hear it," Cato said. "If you don't mind."

Rachel cleared her throat and drummed a little pattern on her knees.

Nina prepared to be assaulted by a warbling, off-key portrayal of notes, or some simple nursery rhyme the girl had learned in school. Rachel hummed a small refrain, and then what came out of her was unexpected: a womanly voice that had either seen considerable practice or was guided by pure, natural ability. In any case, it was a sweet and bitter melody that captured Nina's dark feelings:

Hangman, hangman, slack up your rope,
Oh, slack it for a while.
I looked down yonder, and I seen Pa comin',
He's walked for a many long mile.

Rachel Buell's voice was downright lovely. Unlike Jasmine's rich, earthy tones, Rachel's timbre was like clear crystal, lilting and lively. Like cool, running water on a gentle spring morning.

Oh, Pa. Say, Pa, have you brought me any gold,
Any gold to pay my fee?
Or have you walked these many long miles
To see me on the hangin' tree?

No, son. No, son, I ain't brung you no gold,
No gold for to pay your fee.
But I just walked these many long miles
To see you on the hangin' tree

There was more to the song, but the words couldn't compare to the sweet sound of Rachel's voice. Even as the tears flowed down the girl's face, and her voice cracked at times, she never stopped, and Nina noticed Greta and Cato both watched with tears in their eyes, as well. Everyone else had their eyes shut, and Nina followed suit, wrapped herself around the melody, and closed her eyes against the cruel, brutal world.

Let Rachel cast the shadows away, as unfair a burden as it was for a young girl to bear. Nina was just plain tuckered out. She let herself sink into the lilt and the sway, and swam down into a singsong, dreamless sleep.

CHAPTER TWELVE

*T*HE MOTIONLESS SILENCE WOKE her. The swaying of the wagon, the endless creaks and groans and jarring bumps that could loosen your teeth were gone. The canvas cover was awash in daylight. The smells of stale sweat and old blood lingered. And dust. But they were stopped.

Nina noticed small sounds, then. Snores. Several snores. *Lot better than moans.*

She rubbed her eyes and sat up. Cato and Greta slept back to back, while Pa rumbled steadily in the corner—she'd know that snore anywhere. Buck and Red remained against the front wall, leaning against one another like two blood-stained blood brothers. Rachel lay against Jasmine,

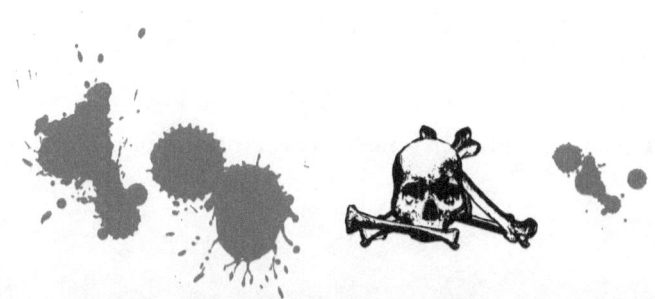

Mathias was asleep sitting up in the same position she'd last seen him, and Manning was curled up on his right side beside her.

She blinked to clear more of the sleep from her caked eyes. *Jesus.*

Everyone was covered in blood; hands and arms, fingernails dipped in red, shirts and dresses stained a deep brown, necks and cheeks smeared with the stuff. All their sins exposed in the light of day. They had the appearance of a pack of murderous bandits fresh off a violent raid, or perhaps a band of gypsies hell-bent on terrorizing the countryside.

If only it were that simple.

She put her fingers on James' neck. Strong pulse. She felt a little better about that. *Thank you, Father.*

Nina held his arm, feeding off his warmth for a moment, basking in the memory of last night *before* all hell broke loose. His arms around her, his kisses on her, him inside her…She'd give anything if this morning would *stay* quiet, filled with peace, in the company of her unhinged, hopeless, slumbering bunch.

Nina smiled and stretched—*holy hell!*—before moving as quiet as she could over the sleeping bodies. Her shoulders and arms were raw and sore, her back full of protest as she stepped down onto the dirt road. She squinted into an overbearing layer of gray clouds, the kind of clouds that were still bright enough to hurt. She waited for her eyes to adjust, looking back up the road and wondering just where in blazes they were.

Nina took off her hat and let her hair play in the breeze that blew across the road, then scratched her crusted scalp.

That was a week's worth of itch, seven days of scum caked on so thick she'd probably never get it off. She lifted her arm and whiffed at her armpit. Smelled like blood. Everything did. Guess she'd become immune to her own stench. She remembered a few nights ago in Truckee when Pa, his ass sticking out of that overturned wagon, had asked if she wanted a dress. She'd kill for a bath and a durned dress right now—as long as she could get her gun belt over it, of course.

She sighed and glanced about. Where in Tarnation were they?

Nina went to see what was happening up front. The horses were still tethered; they snorted and stamped at the sight of her, probably indignant at their poor treatment. George Daggett leaned over in the driver's chair, sleeping sitting up, blood crusted in his hair and over half his face, breathing so deeply you'd have thought the man had never slept before. Same with Mason on the other side—minus the bloody head. Strobridge lay stretched out in the seat, muddy boots hanging over the foot rest, softly snoring, head tossed back, neck exposed to the sky. Nina shuddered. Lucky nothing had come to tear it out. She pictured deadun teeth ripping into that hairy Adam's apple. These assholes hadn't even set a watch, all of 'em easy pickings. *Yup, damn lucky.*

She thought about smacking 'em awake and giving 'em hell, but there was the wind ruffling the grass and the horses making a susurrus with their tails…things felt too peaceable to have to bicker with folks. Instead, she looked down the rutted road, simply wheel-made furrows in the earth that stretched southward for miles, and tracked as the land rose to her right, became scrub-covered hillsides and slim valleys with twisty grooves etched into them. Beyond that, several massive, snow-capped peaks ran away to the west, mountains she'd need Pa's help to name, if they had names at all.

Were those hills filled with deaduns? Working their way over stone and through briar, some of 'em trapped in gullies or ditches, doing their dumb, dead walk until Liao Xu's influence over them waned or they fell to pieces in the oven-dry air.

Nina shook her head. Not something to dwell on when they were sitting in the open, vulnerable. She put her hat back on and glanced the other way, east. More nothing. A scenery of low hills as far as she could see. They'd have to pass Lake Washoe on the way to Carson City. Maybe they hadn't reached it yet. Maybe it was buried somewhere behind those low hills. Or maybe they'd already passed it. Who the hell knew?

A sense of being watched nagged her. Nina scanned the sky, searching the gray for specks of birds or shadowy flying devils—anything that might indicate Liao Xu was on their trail. *You're just waking up*, she thought. Understandably paranoid. But what happened to feeling safer in the daytime?

It's all an illusion. They could think what they wanted, but Liao Xu was coming.

She'd need to visit her *boha gande* soon to learn more about her power—and her limitations. Nina needed to know how to fight Liao Xu. She needed to figure out who and what she was. *But how exactly?*

She headed on back to the rear of the wagon, but fetched

up, fell against the wheel, petrified at the thing watching her from across the road atop a large, curved stone. She hadn't seen it before, had looked right past it. Or maybe she'd not been *willing* to see it and blamed the bleak iron-gray sky.

In any case, there *it* was.

A cyclopean eye, edged with puffy flesh, bulging at her, worming around in its socket as if studying her from assorted angles with a fidgeting, ravenous interest. The whole of its featherless frame, easily more than half her size, was the color of coal, mere skin stretched over bone; only its folded wings sprouted wild, rumpled plumes. Its head swiveled on a thin, flexible neck. A long beak curved downwards, ending in a fine point. The thing's fat, scaled legs were tipped with talons that clicked on the rock whenever it moved. She took note of a festering wound on the left side of its breast near the wing.

Nina was suddenly struck with the image of the unlucky sawmill worker named Christopher, his head plucked off, arcing through the air. Whatever this infernal thing was, she knew it was also Liao Xu. She knew it as surely as she'd ever known anything. Nina straightened, unwilling to let it feed on her fear. "I was wonderin' where you'd got to."

"Were you?" Its voice was every squeaky door she'd ever heard opened at once. Every wagon wheel starved for grease. "We've found each other again, Nina Weaver."

"You're determined, I'll give you that."

"And *you* are very serendipitous."

"Don't know the meaning of that word, but you ever thought maybe we *wanted* you to find us. Ever think about that, you evil fuck?"

The foul critter tilted its dark head. "I do not think so,

Ninataku, Fire Eater. You are terrified of me, even now. As well you should be. Your priest is worn thin, his frail mind unable to understand that I have outgrown him. He is a broken man, waving around his pathetic crucifix and his book of lies, filled with empty words never uttered by his pretend god. What will you do when you are the only one left? When your father can no longer protect you and your lover is a broken sack of flesh?"

Nina pulled her Colt. Probably not worth a damn against this devil, but the weight was reassuring. "Even brave people get scared, but that doesn't keep them from standing up to assholes like you. Hell, I been scared shitless for days, but still managed to carve up a few score of your deaduns and choked up your demon train, too."

The sickly thing shifted on the rock, claws scratching its perch. "I would offer you a place by my side, if I did not dream of skinning you alive, Nina Weaver. But you will have a place in my kingdom, one way or another."

Nina took a step forward. "I don't think so."

"I am coming," it croaked, twisted its head to the north where a gathering of red-hued clouds rolled south across the sky.

"Right now you're *going*." Nina raised her Colt, cocked it, and sighted the squawking thing. She poured her will into the steel, into every grain of black powder that was probably too wet to fire, every hard-packed ball of lead. She imagined doing with one bullet what thirty rounds couldn't do to Rachels' possessed father back at Fort Bluff.

She tried to think of something to say to invoke her *boha gande* and the spirit of the People. Some kind of prayer, something Father Mathias might say to his god, but Nina was no preacher and, truth be told, she didn't have an eloquent bone in her body.

Just let me kill him. Please, just let me do this one blessed thing…

Nina pulled the trigger. A .36 caliber ball flew from the barrel, true to its target. A fine spray of black mist exited the other side of the Liao-thing along with Nina's lead. The beast jerked into the sky, shrieking and caterwauling, shedding plumage as it flew on a wild, wounded course. With a yelp of victory, Nina squeezed the trigger again, this time striking the beast in mid-flight where it plunged to the ground. A quiet rumble of distant thunder, then all was still.

THE DAGGETTS AND STROBRIDGE were cussing and springing up, while the rest of the folks inside the wagon started up like a nest of jackrabbits dogged from the burrow. Nina sensed Liao Xu's spirit exiting the mutilated, deflating corpse of the foul creature. She hadn't killed him, but it felt good all the same.

"He's gone," Nina said.

"Who?" George Daggett truly looked hell-fired. His forehead was swollen and leaking from somewhere beneath his hair line, a dark seepage that looked more like crude than blood.

"Liao paid a visit, and I shot his ass."

"What the hell you talking about?" Strobridge's cold stare stabbed at her, and he looked highly agitated.

Nina pointed off toward where the thing fell. "Have a look."

So Mason, George, Strobridge, Red, Buck, and Cato all headed that way, the latter giving her a wide-eyed look before hurrying after the other men. They strode past the rock and all stared down at the ground, and to abate her curiosity Nina headed that way, as well.

Pa was just now crawling out of the wagon, asking "What now?" as he got down and stood next to Rachel. Nina could see it from a distance away, and the thing was a black lump of bone and tar and really nothing much to look at.

"God in Heaven!" It was Jasmine, and she stood next to Pa and Rachel, her arm raised, pointing at the sky. Those faint crimson clouds from before had turned an angry red, and they were rolling quickly toward them.

"What the hell is it?" Mason asked.

"It's Liao. He's sending a storm." Nina headed back toward the wagon. She needed to see James. And she noticed Mathias was sitting at the wagon's edge, looking gaunt and empty.

"Right," Strobridge said, walking back toward the wagon, as well. "Time to go."

There were a few more questions but Nina just hurried everyone back inside the wagon and was the last to climb in as it started to roll. Everyone crowded around the back port and watched the crimson cloudbank approach. It roiled, one wave of frothy red reaching over another like an ocean of blood in the sky.

Jasmine gazed hard at the approaching menace. Nina gasped. Jasmine's eyes were sunken, dark circles beneath them. Her skin held an ashen pallor. There was no hint of the dark beauty her skin normally radiated.

Nina felt a knot tighten in her guts. "Can I take a look at your neck?"

Jasmine shook her head. Tried a good-natured smile. "No need, I'm fine. Just slept like shit. Woulda been better off staying awake."

Cato pulled his eyes away from the crimson torrent, that *unnatural* motion in the sky. "I think I might be ill," he murmured, turning back inside.

Nina went to check Manning, concerned he hadn't woken up with all this commotion. His pulse was steady, though his skin was clammy. She tried to pour a little water in his mouth, but most of it spilled on the floorboards.

Rachel squeezed in beside her and stared at Manning for a long moment until Nina met her gaze. "He's going to be okay," she told Rachel, though in truth it was more for her own benefit. "We just need to get to Carson City and he'll be okay."

"I heard you talking outside, heard you shoot at…" the girl spoke in barely a whisper, "…*him*."

Nina wasn't sure what to say back to that, so she didn't say anything.

"You're brave," Rachel continued. "I wish I would have been that brave when Ma was—"

Nina shushed her. "No, Rachel. None of us could've done anything for your ma. Hell, we *tried*. And trust me, I ain't no braver than you." She gave in to her instincts, took Rachel's hand, and gave it a squeeze. "I'm not brave, but I am pissed. You know what I mean? You gotta push the fear down and find the fight deep inside of you. We all have it. You gotta find yours."

Rachel nodded, looked at Nina with soulful eyes the

color of bluebells. "Ma would say something like someone's reached their breaking point. Something like that."

"That's right. The breaking point. That's where we gotta be now."

Rachel turned her head away, looked at Jasmine, who stared with a blank, tired expression out the back of the wagon. "What's that thing gonna do when it reaches us?"

Nina shrugged. "I couldn't say. Nothin', I hope."

"Me, too."

"Find the fight inside, okay? 'Cause I have a feelin' we're gonna need you directly."

Rachel bit her lip. Then nodded. "I can. I *will*."

"Good."

"Oh!" Father Mathias slapped his palm lightly against his head, then looked around. His eyes alighted on Nina's pa.

"What is it, Father?" Pa asked, still looking a bit haggard despite a few hours' sleep.

As tired as Pa still looked, the priest's eyes were filled with bloodshot exhaustion. Nonetheless, a smile lit his face. "I think I know what's been giving us away." He pulled the key to the Taiping Jing from his pocket. "Touch this, Lincoln. Tell me I'm not imaging things."

Pa did so, then nodded. "It feels awful warm to the touch. Unusually so. Buck?"

Buck reached out and felt it. "Yup. What's that mean?"

"He's been tracking us through this, I'm sure of it. And it's my fault. I should have bound it from his sight. The thought did not even occur." Mathias sighed. "I feel a fool."

"Is there any way you can bind it *now*?" asked Pa.

"I can, but I'll need a few things." Then he looked directly at Rachel Buell.

T HE PRIEST HAD CALLED her *unbloodied*. Still young enough that her innocence would be powerful against Liao Xu's magic. "She's…pure," he had said.

Upon request, Rachel removed her bonnet, plucked several long strands of her dirty blonde hair, and handed them over to Mathias. They used the sharp point of Nina's knife to get three drops of blood from her palm. Rachel didn't wince when Nina poked her, but she did leave teeth marks in her lower lip.

Everyone in the wagon watched with a range of looks from curious to dubious as Father Mathias rubbed Rachel's blood with his fingers, covering the bejeweled key in sticky, red smears. Then he bound the item with the strands of her hair, tying them gently in a figure eight pattern—an impressive feat considering the wagon jostling about—all the while mumbling prayers and appeals.

"Now, Rachel, touch it and repeat after me: *That innocent blood be not shed in thy land, which the Lord thy God giveth thee for an inheritance, and so blood be upon thee. Amen.*"

Rachel repeated the words, her voice given strength upon uttering the verse. It seemed she was even familiar with the passage, the words flowing so readily from her tongue.

Father Mathias hefted the Taiping Jing key. "There, see. It is entirely invisible to Liao Xu now." He held it out for them to touch.

Nina touched the object and found it be cool, almost cold, in fact.

Pa patted Mathias on the shoulder. He didn't say it, but Nina wagered her father wished Mathias had thought of it sooner.

A minute later, everything darkened, and Rachel squeezed in tight between Nina and Jasmine. Thunder rumbled overhead, and raindrops fell on the canvas. Nina crawled to the back of the wagon and squatted next to Cato, his lower lip aquiver. Something strange about seeing a man that big looking so mighty terrified.

Nina followed his gaze. She gaped at the torrent bearing down on them. The hair on the back of her neck stood up as a violent, ruddy mist chased them, so thick they couldn't see more than twenty yards behind. The overpowering scent of copper and wet dirt pressed in on her.

"*Blod*," Greta whispered in her native tongue. "*Det* är *blod*."

"Yeah, this ain't no normal kinda downpour," Nina said. She focused on the drops of wetness that stained the wagon, her eyes going wide with realization.

It was raining blood.

CHAPTER THIRTEEN

Someone up front yelled "*heyaa!*" and whipped the reins. The wagon picked up speed, hitting ruts and grooves that could flip them at any moment. No one complained.

Nina saw Greta had a case of the shakes.

"Hang on, ya hear?" she said, then knelt next to him, pushing aside a box that had fallen on his feet. She lifted his face, put his arm around her knee. "James." Nina gave his face a gentle pat, but no response. "James!" this time she smacked him on the cheek and was rewarded with a flutter of his eyelids. He moaned.

"Wake up!" Nina shook him, kissed him, shook him

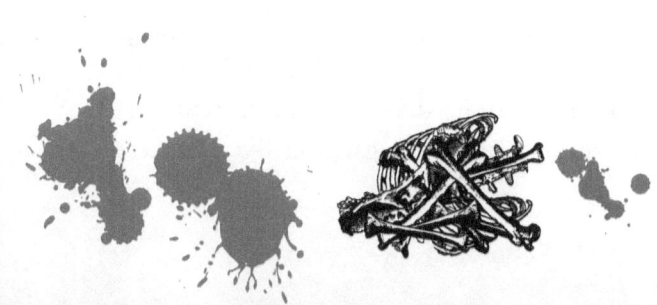

some more, did everything she could to get him moving. After a long minute of trying, Manning jerked awake, his eyes practically spinning before coming to rest on Nina.

"Hey," he croaked. "That's a fair sight."

Nina shook her head. That was the perfect thing for him to say, but the timing was a little off.

Manning sat up, looked all around, winced at the rainfall hitting the canvas cover, finally noticing they were running full chisel. "What? What is…" The wagon hit another rut and cut off the rest of his question.

"Best just to see for yourself." Nina pointed between Cato and Greta, outside the wagon. Manning attempted to move toward the back, but the wagon bounced jarringly, the rear end lifting up and slamming back down. Folks howled as the rear wheels lifted and crashed down a second time, skidding them sideways around a sharp turn. Red Thunder grabbed Manning's coat arm to keep him from tumbling into Mathias, and the priest reached out to steady him.

"Maybe you should just sit," the priest offered.

Manning looked pale. "What the deuce is going on?" He ignored the advice and climbed over Jasmine and Rachel while holding his belly, pushed his way between Cato and Greta.

Nina followed and came up alongside him.

"Well, this don't look good at all," he said.

"No, sir," Cato agreed. "It sure don't."

Nina noticed something else, too. Something horrific that defied explanation. Wherever the blood rain fell, things squirmed up through the earth; brackish tendrils, critters that looked like birds or rats, devious mongrels waddling after them on stunted, crooked legs. Deer-like creatures pulled themselves free from the mud like foals from the hemorrhaging abdomen of the earth, spindly-legged monstrosities bleating and stumbling on their fledgling legs.

George Daggett came down through the flap, covered in wet crimson. He pushed toward the back of the wagon, muscled in beside Nina, and shouted when he saw what followed them, what grew from the ground. "Holeee-shee-it!" He scrambled off, yelling "Faster!" to the drivers. "Faster, goddammit!"

Thunder clamored above them like a giant breathing against the canvas cover, pealing so loud that Rachel and Cato both covered their ears. A thick shower washed over them, then tapered off again. If some of them could have panicked and ran, they would have, Nina knew by the looks on their horrified faces. But there was nowhere to run.

Cato crawled away, knocked Father Mathias aside, and climbed over crates of food to cower in the corner beside Red Thunder. The Indian looked at the black man with a stoic expression, the only one of them who did not look rattled. He sat calmly, tomahawk in hand, while, next to him, Buck fiddled with his hunting knife. Pa merely looked at her.

Rachel and Jasmine took up the floor where Manning had been laying just a few minutes ago. The girl held Jasmine's head and stroked her hair nervously as the black woman wept into her lap. Nina turned back and saw the unsure look on Greta's face, caught somewhere between joining Cato or jumping out the back to certain death.

Mathias clung to a wagon rib, holding on as they lurched again. "This is quite the predicament."

"Is that what you call something like this, Father?" Nina

ground her jaw, her mind working to figure out how they might get out of this.

"More like a catastrophe," Manning said through clenched teeth, hand still on his stomach wound.

The wagon drove into something thick, as if tearing through a field of tall grass. Nina peered down as the very earth rebelled to stop them. Those snaky tendrils, now four and five feet long, waved like thick, flexible saplings along the road. It was those things grabbing at the wheels, no doubt tripping up the horses.

Nina pulled her knife free. "We'll have to stand and fight soon."

Manning put his arm around her shoulders and hugged her to him. "You got any magic left in you?"

"I don't know." And that was the honest truth. Her *boha gande* hadn't come to her rescue at Ramdohr's sawmill, but neither had she tried to summon him or any of the People. Just how would she do it? The whole incident on the train felt like a misty dream lingering at the edges of her waking mind, seeping away.

If magic worked the way Father Mathias described it, then it was unpredictable, about as reliable as dumb luck. All one could do was coax it. There wasn't any real command. It was all just fucking happenstance.

But, hell, she had nothing to lose for trying. Nina closed her eyes, focused on Manning's arm around her, on the drums and voices of the Shoshone, listened for the *thrum* beneath all the other sounds, tried to feel it inside as if it had never gone away, had never left her, but only quieted. Nina for courage.

Thrum.

She pictured a spring shower, a welcome rain, washing away the earthen debris, all the detritus of winter. Suddenly, the blood rain didn't seem so terrible, despite the hungry things in it. Any other power she might tap remained latent. No wave of godliness to wash the evil away, no blessed lump of coal to kill this storm.

Yet, she sensed the spirit world awaited.

Thrum.

Their progress slowed. Why?

The wagon finally ground to a halt, wheels seizing. Nina opened her eyes.

There was only the rain, the complaints of the horses, the gagging reek of coppery blood—and those *things* slithering around out there, those stumbling, bleating beasties.

The Daggetts and Strobridge piled into the wagon from the seat above, soaked in blood rain. Strobridge wiped his hands on his pants. "The horses are caught, and so are the wheels. We've got to go out there and cut ourselves free." He looked at Cato, cowering in the corner. "What's wrong with him?"

George regarded everyone from behind a bloodstained mask. "We got maybe ten bullets," he said, and closed the cylinder on his pistol.

Cato seemed to have roused from his sniveling after having drawn some attention. "I still got my peavey hook." He grabbed up the hook-spear thing from beneath a crate against the sideboard.

"Greta's got an ax, Red his tomahawk, we got knives," Nina said. "But we'll need someone ready to drive soon as we cut loose."

"That's me," Strobridge said. "Let's not wait around." He

climbed back up into the seat.

The rain had tapered off to a drizzle, a red mist hanging over the road. Whatever beasts stalked them remained just out of view, but their menacing intentions were palpable.

Buck and Red Thunder were the first ones out. "James, you're still moving slow. You stay with Pa and the girls, okay?"

"You're going out there?"

"I gotta help."

Cato was the next one clambering out, saying, "Holy Jesus, protect us."

Nina leapt out of the wagon before Manning could say anything else, and landed with a *splash* in a puddle of rust-colored mud. Something swiped at her boot and she kicked it, then swept left. The wagon wheels were indeed wrapped up in the thick, veiny, stems. Some had been torn to pieces, caught up in the spokes and adding to the obstruction. Nina took the front wheel and began clearing the mess, plucking out gruesome slabs of unholy flesh, holding her breath against the stench, and quickly cutting anything that wrapped around her boot.

Cato worked on the rear wheel with his hook, face all twisted up in a grimace of disgust. If they weren't in such a gruesome situation, Nina might have laughed.

"I'm going to try to free up the horses," she said. "Watch this wheel if any more grow up. And work quick—we ain't got time to pussyfoot around."

"Yes'm." Cato nodded, flashed a flummoxed smile, which looked gruesome as hell through the veneer of blood on his dark skin. He hooked away more gray-fleshed creepers as Nina trotted to the front.

The horses weren't in horrible shape, all things considered. More terrified than anything. They sat in the red mud, legs tangled in wormy vines.

"Easy, now," she told the quaking beast as she worked. Realizing they were being freed, the horses struggled harder against their bonds. One jerked free and stood. George showed up from the other side of the wagon to help her with the others.

He shook his head as he worked, as if constantly snapping out of a daze. The top of his head had gotten a pregnant swell, like a walnut growing just beneath his skin. Couldn't even keep his hat on anymore, and his forehead had taken on a charcoal tone. The man looked two shades from dead.

He chuckled, a sick shake in his voice. "I thought I seen everything..."

"Yeah, I know. You were at Shiloh. But I wasn't, so don't go talkin' shit about it."

"I wasn't talkin' *shit*. Just sayin', I *seen* some shit, but nothin' to top *this* here shit. This is what I'd call royal shit. I'd call this here, I'd call it shit of epic proportions." George yanked a squeezing tendril away from the horse's neck and sliced it. "Shit, shit, shit, and more fuckin' shit!"

George bemoaned a lot, about as incessant as anyone she's ever known, but Nina could understand why he made a good soldier. Steadfast, adept with his hands, wiry, and competent for the most part.

Nina smiled. "I'd call this a four-course meal of shit."

"I'd call this a wagon chock-full of *shit*." He emphasized the last, clearly enjoying the sound of the word.

With both horses up, George called for Strobridge. "Let's

go!" The railroad boss flicked the reins, and the horses were more than happy to oblige.

"A platter of shit sandwiches," Nina said, chuckling.

"You're disgusting," George told her from the other side of the horses. "Wait, is that squirrel shit or human shit?"

"Human." The answer out before she could think about it.

"Yup, you're disgusting."

"Squirrel shit ain't?"

"I reckon I'd eat squirrel shit if I had to."

Nina shook her head, stifling a laugh, as they guided the horses at a good clip through the steady, blood drizzle. The road was far too treacherous to take it any faster, some places having been completely washed away by the deluge. Things wandered in and out of Nina's view, swimming in a mist, which did not want to give up its secrets just yet. Nina fretted. She'd rather Liao just do what he was gonna and get it over with. Tired and mangy with barely a smidgen of firepower, they'd be sitting ducks for him when he decided to make his play. She was sick of waiting.

Like an answered prayer from some god of ill luck, the rain picked up. The slimy tentacles slithered out of the ground in thick clumps, drawing energy from the morbid downpour. Strobridge flicked the reins harder, but it was too late. Thicker this time, the wormy tendrils twined through the spokes and wrapped up the wheels faster than they could be cut.

Cato cried out in frustration as he strained against the fleshy onslaught. Nina went to his aid. Before she could reach him, wood groaned and the axle splintered. Nina started to cut the stems but changed her mind and threw her weight against Cato who'd partially slid beneath the wagon. He pulled his legs clear just as a pained groan shook the heavy wooden frame. The wheels shattered inward, and the wagon bed smashed to the ground.

The horses went the same way, pulled over by the weight of the wagon and the insistent tug of the vines. Covered in tentacles, worn out and scared, the poor animals fell to the ground and were pinned. They screamed as their legs snapped like twigs beneath the tentacles' brutal strength. The vines strangled them in the bloody mud, their muted *neighs* spilling out as moist rattles.

"Christ!" George yelled. He shot one of the horses. "You sonofabitch! Fuck you!"

"Don't waste your bullets!" Strobridge bellowed.

George ignored him and shot the remaining horse.

"Goddammit!" Strobridge yelled.

"Let's get inside," Mason hollered at his brother, his sentence punctuated by thunder.

They all piled in, clambering over one another in a not-so-orderly fashion, knocking aside what was left of the supply boxes in their haste. The ground quaked, the wagon bed shook, and a tendril shot up through the wood. It swiped at George amidst a spray of jagged splinters. The Reb threw his hands over his head, screaming into his shirt. "They're gonna tear the wagon to pieces. I'd rather be taken by a blasted Yank than one of these...*things*. What the fuck are we gonna do?"

Rachel grabbed a tin can from a spilled crate and hurled it at the tendril, then cried out in surprise as something wrapped around her ankle. Manning reached to help her, while Jasmine sat quietly in the middle, staring out the back of the wagon with dark tears streaming down her dark cheeks.

Nina couldn't get to Rachel. She twisted back and forth, knife in hand as more things wiggled up through the floor—there was little she could do. Soon they'd be pulled to the ground just like those horses, torn to pieces and dragged off, buried, gone like they'd never been born.

Mathias leapt up, a determined look on his face. "God willing, none of you will be taken today." The priest clutched a wiggling tendril in each hand and shouted in a voice given volume by his conviction. "I will tell you about the Revelation of Jesus Christ, which God gave unto Him to show unto His servants' things which must shortly come to pass." The things squealed in Mathias's hands, grayish skin turning ashen; yet, they wrapped around Mathias's wrists and sought to pull him down. "I am Alpha and Omega," Mathias shouted, "the beginning and end, sayeth the Lord, who is, was, and will always be, the Almighty."

Mathias lifted his arms, stretching those tendrils taut. "While we may not be worthy of you, oh Lord, with not your mark upon our heads, please have mercy and send your tenth angel to seal up those things which this evil has uttered, as the tenth will do at the End of Days." The priest lifted his eyes, gazed up through the ripped canvas to the ruby sky, and shouted into the rain. "It is not your right to pass judgment, Liao Xu. That right is reserved for the Lord!" With that, the slimy tentacles in his hands dried up, hardening, then flaked apart like ancient parchment.

Father Mathias continued his versing. Whatever wicked tendril he grabbed withered and fell away, disintegrating into clouds of dust. Soon, the wagon was clear, and Mathias stepped through the rubble of the wagon, over Greta, past

Jasmine, and over the broken rear gate.

The Black Robe priest stepped outside. He fell to his knees and punched his hands into the gunk. An upheaval shook the entire road, sending everyone in the wagon sprawling, then Mathias swooned and keeled over in the mud. All was quiet but the kisses of red rain against the shredded canvas cover.

M ATHIAS LOOKED PALE, BUT alive. He sat in the mud, eyes glazed, while Pa and Buck leaned over him, checking him over. They had been the first ones over the rear gate, and because it felt like a tomb inside the wagon, Nina was the next out.

Her boots squelched in the red mud as she scanned the mist's edge, her head spinning. Then she saw it, a wide circle of ground all around the wagon, devoid of everything but mud, the wagon's husk, and the dead horses. No rain fell within the circle, *nothing* moved or wriggled or slithered. It was as if the land had been cleansed—made sacred by Mathias's prayers.

She wanted to feel relief, but Liao Xu would not give up so easy. He still had 'em dead to rights, and nobody had a blamed clue how to turn the tables on the sonofabitch. *How do you chase a damn ghost?*

"Everyone stay within the circle," Mathias muttered.

"The circle?" Cato asked, climbing out from beneath the broken ribs of the wagon bed. He assisted Rachel up and over the canted gate, then took up his hook spear. He looked like a mountain of a man next to the girl, his shirtless torso glistening black and red.

Nina indicated the circle's edge with a sweep of her hand, and folks took in the gesture, realization dawning quicker for some more than others, but they all got it soon enough. They gathered outside the wagon…and waited. How long, Nina couldn't tell. The sun was up there somewhere, hard to say where, lost behind all that roiling gray and red.

They couldn't very well charge out into the rain or leave the protective circle. Even if they knew where to find Liao Xu—the *real* Liao Xu—what would they do then? How could they defeat him?

Manning came to stand beside her, still holding his gut gingerly, pale as a ghost, but his expression hard—a sort of ragged indignation. It was a look she'd grown to appreciate. "I reckon everyone's out of ideas."

"We *been* out of ideas for a while, James."

He nodded. "So…reckon we just wait it out."

"I don't know." Nina shook her head. "I don't know…"

"You still got a line in on those spirit people of yours?"

She sighed. "My *spirit people* ain't all that receptive of late."

"Have you tried?"

She looked at him, trying to hide her sudden annoyance. "What do you think?"

"Have you…maybe thought about talking to Red about what to do? He knows all about that…I don't know… that *stuff*."

"I've shut my eyes a dozen times. I've screamed at the sky. Red Thunder…he's helped guide me as best he can, but ain't nothing he can do now. Even *if* the *boha gande* heard my question loud and clear, I never seem to get answers anyone'd call straight. It's always a goddamn puzzle."

"Maybe you should clarify your needs better, or be more demanding…"

"And maybe you should mind your goddamned business and not preachify about shit you got no fuckin' clue about." Nina pursed her lips as she looked at him. On the inside she regretted her words even as she was saying them— and now even more so considering the look that spread across Manning's face, conflicted with being dressed down and bruised at the same time in front of the Daggetts, Strobridge, and Rachel, who all seemed to be paying attention now.

James' eyes fastened on her, his jaw muscles tightened.

"Look," she said, peering up into his face, wanting to ease the tension away. "It ain't that easy. Hell, I just figured out I had this…whatever it is. What would you do if all the white folk in the world started knocking on your dreams, tellin' you to climb that there mountain without telling you why? Or why you should be the one to do it?"

James shook his head and sighed. The tension fell away from him a little, his stance softening. "I'm sorry. I…I shouldn't have said it that way. I'm not a hundred percent, Nina. You came through for us before. You'll do it again. I don't doubt it."

"That's just it, James." Nina looked away, looked at her pa and Buck, helping Mathias to his feet. "I ain't comin' through for us this time. I feel empty."

James said nothing, he just took her hand in his and squeezed it near to painful, yet it felt just about right. Like any man, he had the capability to be a real horse's ass, but other times, he did exactly what the moment called for.

"Guess they made up," she heard Mason say to someone;

likely George, but whatever words that followed after she ignored.

They stood in the rain for some time, leaning shoulder to shoulder, until Nina stopped looking for anything that might come out of the mist, until she stopped caring what happened next, just happy for the contact, content to soak up the warmth James Manning passed on through to her with that simple touch.

The silence was broken by Greta Ramdohr, who'd been squatting on the wagon's tailgate with her ax in her lap. "What's that?" She pointed down the road. A man limped through the rain, one leg dragging wretchedly behind him.

As the figure neared, she could see it was a deadun, but there was something familiar about him. Nina's guts roiled once it came into plain view at the edge of the blood mist.

It was Woodie.

CHAPTER FOURTEEN

*L*ESTER WOODRUFF TEETERED ON unsteady legs. His mouth was a dry slit of swollen flesh. Hair and bone still stuck up from where the bullet had exited his head, giving him the ruffled look of someone who'd just rolled out of bed. His eyes were wider apart than they were in life, on account of his skull being all deformed from the blast. Those cocked-up eyes focused on Manning.

"Why you do thith, Mathing? I dun nuthin' to you." The voice was a croak, attempting to sound human, but with awkward little pauses between each fucked-up word spilling out from between those broken teeth. "Juth wan' folk to 'thpec me. Juth wan' akthep-enth."

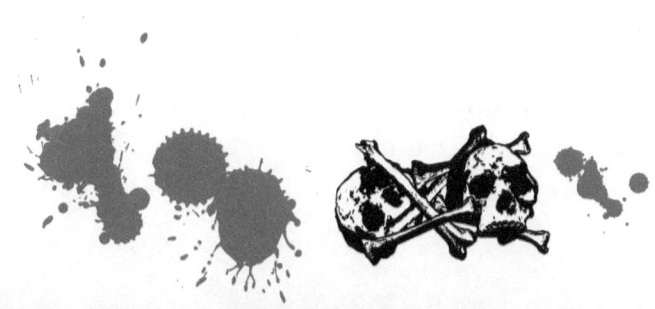

Sweat-soaked and looking exhausted, Manning swallowed hard. His teeth gnawed at his bottom lip, hand still against his stomach. Nina noticed fresh wetness there.

"Liao is just fuckin' with our heads," Nina said to him. "That ain't Woodie."

Manning nodded a little too vigorously, wiped his coat sleeve across his mouth. "Right."

"You seen better days there, Woodie," Strobridge said from his place near the wagon. "Sorry about your luck. I always kinda liked you…some."

"That ain't Woodruff." Pa took a few steps toward the deadun. "Are you?"

"Pa, no," Nina said. "Don't."

Woodie's pale eyes flickered at her, then at her father. The deadun's head turned to the side, showed its teeth in what seemed to be a grin, but hard tellin'. It clacked its chompers, then made a noise like a dying man's last gasp.

"Mister Xu, seems we've had a misunderstanding since all this started," Pa said, hands out in a placating gesture. "We didn't mean to get in your way, and I think you might admit maybe you've underestimated us some. We've cost you lots of…of your troops, so…I guess we've all lost something. What say we call a truce? End the fighting for a spell."

The voice that came from Woodie's broken mouth was no longer his, but Liao's. "I have lost nothing that cannot be replaced. The corpses of the world are at my beck and call. I am a lord of realms you cannot even begin to fathom, and I have waited long enough. I will take divine pleasure in your sequestration into my ranks. It is quite a painful process if undertaken while one is yet alive."

Pa fell to his knees, the act as unnatural to Nina as the deadun standing before them. "Won't you have mercy? Please…my daughter, she—"

"My only mercy is to ask one last time. Any of you may join me at my right hand. Or my left. Even behind me would be more desirable than your present position." Liao chuckled through Woodie's mouth. "Make your choice! Will you join me in building my new world? Or do you prefer to see what awaits you in the mist?"

No one spoke, although Nina expected them to, twice over in the case of the Daggetts and Strobridge. She kept her hand on her Colt just in case.

"Not even you, Mister Strobridge?"

Strobridge gazed around at the motley group. His eyes lingered on Jasmine, cowering in the wagon's darkness. The railroad boss shook his head, smiled his shitty grin, and raised his middle finger. "I choose this, you piece of shit."

The deadun chuckled, then, "And what of you, Thomas? I see you hiding back there."

The priest looked white as a sheet and weak as a foal calf. He needed Buck and Cato both to lean on, just to remain standing. "Let us finish this terribly long chapter, Liao. Nobody is going to join you in this madness. You have damned yourself for all eternity…"

"You have been a worthy adversary, Thomas. I will reserve a special place in my new world for you as one of my heavenly subjects." Woodie stepped back into the mist as the edges stirred in agitated swirls. "You are correct. This chapter should have ended days ago. Now your time has finally arrived. Let us close the book."

Nina heard George murmur, "Maybe we shoulda

enlisted, Mase."

Out of the corner of her eye she saw Mason punch George in the shoulder. "Don't matter what side we're on. The war should have taught you that, ya moron. Only thing a man can do is die the way he wants. That's the only real choice we got."

"Just tryin' to buy a little more time. One more shot of whiskey, one more poke..." George laughed. "Damn, I'd provender one of my beans for one last glorious piece o' snatch."

Nina caught George's glance. "Don't look at me."

"You can look at me," Rachel said, and despite the circumstances blood rushed to her cheeks.

George peered at her as if taking the girl seriously, causing Nina to bite her tongue. They were about to be in the shitstorm of their lives, she reckoned, so words didn't much matter none anymore.

She noticed Strobridge fishing around in a tool box affixed to the side of the wagon. He pulled out a chisel and hammer and seemed to test their weight, before rejoining the group. "Arm yourselves, everybody," the boss man said.

That's what it had come down to. Fighting for their lives with wood chopping axes and hand tools.

As one, the group formed a tentative unit at the rear of the wagon. Nina stood between Pa and Manning. They were marred with fear and doubt—Nina glanced to her right and left and caught glimpses in everyone's eyes: the Daggetts' with nervous-set jaws; Strobridge, licking his lips and gazing everywhere at once; Red Thunder and Buck, tense, weapons at the ready; Mathias, gaunt and seemingly lost in a haze; Rachel, wide-eyed, clutching a broken board as her only means of defense; Jasmine, still lingering inside, near comatose and likely sick with fever; Manning, determined, but his posture was weak with exhaustion and blood loss; Cato looked nervous, eyes darting about on his blood-crusted face and twisting the haft of his spear-hook; and Greta, who wanted so badly to be brave, but could just as easily high-tail it soon as she saw whatever was coming.

And what could she say about Pa? She looked down at the bloody mud-stains on the knees of his trousers, thought of him begging Liao Xu for her life. She put her arm around his waist and gave him a squeeze.

Red Thunder and Buck stepped to the fore, side-by-side. They clapped one another on the shoulders and readied knife and tomahawk; blood brothers to the end.

Nina fed off their energy. She growled at the group, "Hey! Let's make the bastard pay."

When they didn't immediately give her their attention, she pulled her gun and shot one into the sky. The waft of black powder smoke beat back the stench of rot from the blood-soaked ground. The acrid smoke was almost comforting, for it had been black powder and lead that had mostly kept them alive till now.

George answered her. "Look, I ain't afraid to die, but we ain't gonna win this. There's, like, *ten thousand* of them fuckin' things out there."

"Then let's make that bastard pay with blood!" she yelled at him.

Red Thunder glanced back over his shoulder at her. "*Alignalghi* means shaman, but you are also *daigwhani*." The Shoshone word for *leader*. "Lead us, Fire-Eater."

Nina nodded at Red, then closed her eyes…yet her sight remained. Through lids as transparent as glass, she watched the ten thousand things approach through the fine, red mist. Ten thousand cawing, crooning things. Things stitched from vine and twisted grass, things re-fleshed on the bones of animals long ago gone and buried in the great basin. Things she wished she could *unsee.*

Yet, even as she clutched her knife and waited for the shambling forms to close, she was slipping from the world. Her color faded, dissolved with every breath. And the world faded alongside her, like the stitches of some great tapestry unraveling.

A crack of thunder shook her soul, and Nina popped out of one world and into another. Flutes filled her head, her senses alive with them; she smelled the echo of sound, tasted the melody, felt the vibrato in her bones.

A breath of honeysuckle touched her cheek.

Nina sobbed. "I'm home."

"Welcome, Ninataku. You have journeyed long in such a short time. How do you feel?" A familiar voice. The *boha gande.* His old form was seated before a simple fire, hands on his knees, two tall urns standing one at each shoulder.

Nina sat down across from him, grinning, barely able to contain her relief. She was still covered in days of gore, her bones ached, and her head hurt, but she was here, surrounded by love and warmth and safety. "I feel good."

"What about your companions?"

"About to die. All of us. In fact, they're probably dying now. And I'll die as soon as you boot me out of here." Nina frowned. "My heart feels like it's being torn apart, yet hard as a piece of ice. Does that make sense?"

The shaman took the urn on his left shoulder, began filling a bowl. "You've seen much for one so young. And you have come through many times where others would have failed. Do not worry, Ninataku. Time is a lazy river here, it courses slowly. We could remain what would feel to you an hour, yet only a minute or two will have passed on the other side."

"I don't think they have a minute."

The *boha gande* nodded. "Then our business must conclude sooner than later, one way or another."

"Our business?"

He offered her the bowl. "Anything rushed becomes business. Drink."

She did. Warm tea, a hint of orange. Sweet. Her gut welcomed it as she gulped. She was ashamed to discover she had drained the bowl. She handed it back empty. "Sorry."

"They make more, Ninataku."

Nina wiped her bloody sleeve across her chin. "Is there anything can be done, *boha gande?*"

"Indirectly, I can provide you with a way." The shaman's visage burned all catawampus in the firelight, filled with a pride Nina hadn't seen in those ancient eyes before. "Daughter, you have earned a spirit guide, should you accept it."

"Why wouldn't I?"

"As you may know, most spirit guides are the spirits of animals who return to befriend and protect the People, to guide them when they think they have no one to turn to. They help us make the right decisions when the wrong ones lead to darkness. A warrior always receives a special spirit guide, one to protect him as he protects the Land."

"Red Thunder told me somethin' like that."

The Shaman's voice took on an ominous tone, as if he wanted to make sure she understood. "There are other spirit guides. They are *anirniit*; powerful entities who were once real people. They are willing to forego the spirit world in order to touch a special person. Usually, it is because of a great need, a great hardship."

"I reckon this hardship's reasonably great," Nina said.

The *boha gande* nodded his head once in a barely perceptible motion. "The Land has never been more threatened in a hundred hundred lifetimes."

Nina sensed the shaman's reluctance to pass along this powerful spirit to her. "And this entity...it wants to help me?"

Again, that nearly imperceptible nod. "But it will always bring you pain."

"I can handle pain."

The *boha gande's* big, dark eyes became sad. They measured her, searching Nina's soul for something. Nina felt a sudden flash of anger. He didn't *want* her to be worthy. Didn't want her representing the People, *her* People...her tribe. Well, he could judge if he wanted, but let him come out with it. Let him be straight. "If I ain't worthy, then pray tell who *is?* Who must I follow?"

"Easy, Ninataku. You do not hunger for the power yourself, but would be willing to follow another in order to bring peace back to the Land." He gave her a yellowed grin, opened his arms. "There is none *more* worthy."

Humming in his old, withered voice, the shaman recited a delicate incantation, just a few simple words with a deep inflection, which twisted into a slightly higher pitch, down to a rhythm she could barely hear. He sighed, his breath passing over Nina like winter wind, carrying the scents of pine needles and dead leaves, wet logs and snow. The *boha gande* closed his arms.

"It is done."

Nina stared at her hands, searched her mind. She looked up, confused. "I don't feel no different."

"So you say."

He filled the bowl again, this time from the other urn. This particular vessel was dyed black, lacking a single inscription or carving. He held the bowl out to her. "Another gift. A new name, should you accept."

"A new name ain't necessary. The next deadun ain't gonna ask my name when it tries to feed on my face."

"This name, you will want."

Nina took the bowl, sniffed it, and glanced up. "Any kind of ill side effects you want to tell me about? My teeth gonna fall out or anything?"

"You must have faith."

Nina thought hard on his words. If she drank this sludge she would never be the same again...might never live like a regular person. Why her? Why not Red Thunder? Or even Pa, who had a wagonload more faith than she ever had. Hell, why not James Manning?

No, she took that back. She'd not want Manning doing what she was about to do.

Life wasn't fair. And there were consequences to everything. Folks made sacrifices when they had to.

Nina sighed and tilted the bowl back, gulped down the dark fluid. It had the consistency of gravy, but tasted like licorice candy. She wasn't all that fond of licorice.

A smile played across the shaman's wrinkled cheeks.

"What is it, *boha gande*? You seem...amused'," she asked after she'd swallowed.

"The spirit world is not devoid of irony, and amusement at said ironies."

"And this particular one?" Nina groaned. She'd known there would be consequences.

His gray-covered head turned up. "I know the man you face, this Liao Xu."

"You fought him?"

"I *still*...fight him."

"Yeah, I suppose you do."

"It is time, Ninataku."

"That's it?"

"That is it. Go back now. To your companions."

Nina stood, gripped her knife, and readied herself to gut the next unfriendly thing she saw. Feeling a spark of ornery, she winked at the shaman. "Last chance to let me stay."

The *boha gande* chuckled. "Staying is easy, Ninataku, Fire Eater. Ninataku, *Shadow Shaper*. It is the going that is always hard."

CHAPTER FIFTEEN

GRETA RAMDOHR SCREAMED IN Nina's face. A string of spit hung from the woman's lower lip. She coughed, blood spotting her lips. Nina caught her, looked over her shoulder at the thing that had jammed its antler through Greta's back and ribs. Hooves stomped on her legs.

The rotted mule deer snorted out a cloud of maggot-ridden, fly-infested discharge. Squirming shapes flung past Nina's face. The beast was big, probably close to three-hundred pounds, and a deadly combination of strong and clumsy. She clutched the base of one of its antlers before it could jerk away and take pieces of Greta with it. Nina yelled and yanked with all her strength, bent its neck down, and

plunged her knife in its eye. It twisted as it fell, dropping atop them and eliciting a scream from Greta. Then the woman went dead silent.

Don't bleed out, Nina thought as she pushed herself free through the red muck. She knew better than to hope.

The rest of the world was a ruinatious mess of noise and blood and mud. The red rain was falling again, and Liao's perversions were everywhere. She got to her feet, while to her right, Cato wrestled with some large bear-looking thing. It stood on its hind legs, the black man's handy hook-spear sunk into its neck while its rotted teeth worried into the Cato's meaty shoulder. They danced in a screaming, moaning cacophony, while fat-bodied rats clung to Cato's trousers, gnawing at the cloth to get inside. He pulled his spear out of the beast and stabbed the spiked end into it again.

Past them, Nina saw George Daggett backed up to the wagon by something she imagined hadn't walked the earth in her lifetime, probably not a score of lifetimes. The rotted reptile had a matted feathery crest and was a head taller than George, and it snapped at him with needle-like teeth. The Reb screamed and jabbed at it with his knife, trying to keep the thing away.

A desperate glance around, Nina couldn't see Pa. No time. She had to focus.

"Spirit warriors of the Land—" she began, then something slammed into her from behind, driving the breath from her lungs. She rolled, scrambled, stabbed, and kicked as something sought to tear out her throat.

Nina flipped on her back and held the thing at bay with one arm while she slashed at it with her blade. It was some kind of mountain cat, or what *used* to be one. It moved awkwardly, stilted, as if hastily thrown together...or *still* coming together. Who knew? Nina almost suffocated from the sheer, rotting weight of it.

"...show me your knives, your spears..." she hissed through clenched teeth. She cut the large cat across its blood-matted neck, nearly slicing her own thumb off, immersing herself in gouts of deadun meat and blood. The thing yawled, hissed fetid air into her face. Nina gagged and steeled her stomach.

"...let the enemy feel the sharp edge of our wrath!"

It swatted Nina's knife from her hand with a large, bony paw. She covered her head, pushed with her knees, trying to fend off those deadly, snapping jaws. She screamed at it, punched it, tried to get hold of the cat's big skull long enough to put her fingers into whatever holes she could find. But it was too damn strong.

Its teeth touched her flesh...

...and then a shadow passed over them, blocking out the gray sky. The weight lifted from her chest, and suddenly she could breathe. Nina coughed and pushed herself up with an elbow, wiped the gunk from her eyes, and gaped.

The shadow loomed over her. An inky black, muscled warrior, covered in nightshade deerskin, held the undead cat by the scruff of its neck, the big feline twisting and swiping with those fat forepaws. The warrior's eyes glinted like onyx as he drew a blade across the cat's throat, finishing the cut Nina started. The rotted corpse dropped while its head jutted skyward, the shadow's dark hand buried in its blood-wet fur. The warrior howled and yipped, teeth like chips of coal, then bounded off, the tar-dipped feathers of his headdress bouncing.

Nina slowly stood, watched as more shadows formed; they were like scattered motes of dust at first, then everywhere. Soon, the churning mist was filled with warcries. Ax and spear divided Liao Xu's unholy ranks. Black arrows split deadun skulls.

Nina, realizing just how far she'd been driven from the wagon, stumbled back in that direction while the pitched fighting raged all around. She had to be careful lest she become a sudden, unwilling participant. She hadn't the strength to fight anymore. She only wanted to get back and find Pa…and Manning and Rachel and Jasmine and Red…just whoever else was alive.

A skirmish tore across her path. An upright thing, another man-sized mockery of a lizard like the one that was attacking George, dragged three shadow warriors behind it, its powerful legs sinking sickle-shaped claws into the mud. Head long and narrow and filled with needle teeth, it reminded Nina of a skull she'd seen once in a Goshute medicine man's tent. It moaned and hissed and snapped at the shadows, but was finally brought down with a splash.

Nina hurried for the wagon, hoping to throw herself against its side. One of the shadow warriors—*her* warriors—careened by, swinging at a feathery blur in the air. The flapper snapped the warriors' head off with its toothy beak.

Or did it?

Nina blinked as the headless warrior caught the thing by its legs and yanked it from the sky, then its head coalesced back into form. Nina inspected the battlefield, saw it was happening elsewhere. Like true shadows, her fighters faded to translucence at will, drifting between worlds as blows that would have been fatal simply passed through them.

Even so, some fell. Caught in mortal combat, they were bit into, held in this world while swarms of deaduns covered them. Nina wondered what happened to their souls; whether they returned to the Shadow Lands or went to some other, horrible place. She felt an icy stab in her chest each time one of them faded away.

Still, the tide was turning. The undead horde was falling, quite literally, to pieces.

Nina grabbed Greta Ramdohr's still form by the ankle and pulled her along the muddy ground until she reached the wagon. She bent, checked the woman for a pulse, and frowned at the result. Fifteen feet away, Cato was on his knees stabbing the re-fleshed bear repeatedly in the neck and skull. She blinked and watched him plunge his spear down over and over, sending pieces of bone and loose rot flying.

"It's dead," Nina told him. But Cato went on, shouting incoherently.

Red Thunder stood out away from the wagon, drenched head to toe in red with piles of deaduns all around him, his chest heaving, tomahawk in one hand, knife in the other, waiting almost eagerly for more enemies.

George sat against the sunken frame, his hands resting on drawn-up knees, the dead reptile laying still. He nudged it with the toe of one boot, then just stared at the ground.

"Pa!" she belted out.

"Over here…" She found him sitting on the other side of the wagon, miraculously alive. His eyes looked up at her approach, and a faint smile touched his lips, his teeth the only part of him that wasn't red. Nina dropped to her knees and they hugged. Pa held her tight, and they shared the silence. All the deaduns were gone or silenced, hopefully forever this time.

James Manning ambled up from somewhere. He rested his hand on Nina's shoulder. "Rachel's missing…and Greta's dead."

"I know."

"Thought you were, too. Dead…"

She got to her feet and gave him a wry smile. "Not your lucky day, is it?"

"Nina girl, it's the damned luckiest day of my life." He pulled her into a blood-soaked embrace.

After a few seconds, while James still held her, Nina opened her eyes and peered at Red Thunder. The Indian walked around, aimless-like, his expression twisted in savage wonderment as he glanced about, trying to unriddle the shadows. Nina shared his wonder. She had no idea where they would go once their purpose was complete. Although, she thought that time might be soon, for a weariness had woven itself into her heart and mind. When she was done, so would they be.

Red gazed at Nina, watching.

The thing that was Lester Woodruff hobbled at the edge of the mist, catching Nina's eye. Red tracked her gaze, spied the deadun in the murk as well, gimp foot sloshing through the bloody mud.

"Woodie," Nina said, breaking their embrace.

James pulled back and looked where she indicated. He started to go after Liao's puppet, but Red Thunder let loose a warcry and charged. The Indian buried his ax in Woodie's skull and kicked the limp husk to the ground.

Manning squinted at the scene, his whole face bunched up.

Nina felt like she should say something to help alleviate some of whatever he was feeling about Woodie's demise and ultimate fate, but as her lips parted a low voice interrupted them.

"She has it..."

They looked to see Father Mathias lurching on his elbows from the guts of the crushed wagon. Pa got up with a grunt and went to help the priest. Nina and Manning joined him, the three of them helping Mathias to stand.

The priest's mouth worked, but his words were faint.

"What's that, Father?" Pa asked, leaning forward.

Mathias repeated himself, and this time they heard him clear as day: "You've got to stop her. She has the *key*."

CHAPTER SIXTEEN

CATO INSISTED ON STAYING behind with Greta's body. The big man had her laid out and cleaned her face with a torn bit of cloth he'd found inside the wagon. He was smoothing her bloody hair back and saying, "Poor Greta…ya'll didn't deserve all this…" as the rest of them ventured outside the protective circle.

They'd left George, as well. He was half out of it, that weird sludge still leaking from his head. Pa and Manning eased him inside the shoddy cover of the wagon and he barely protested except to say, "get offa me" a time or two, but not with any real conviction.

They found Strobridge about fifty yards away, sitting

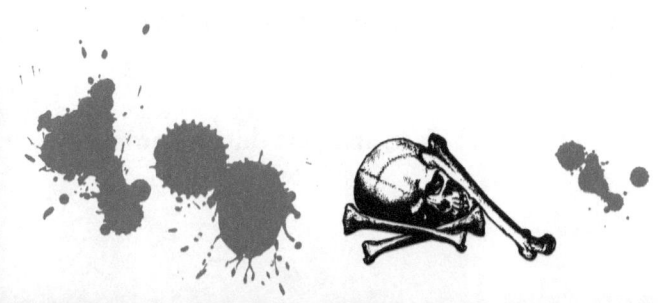

on a bloody carcass. He had his coat off and was using the inside of it to wipe the gore from his face and beard. The dead mule deer he was using as a chair had half its skull exposed, its head twisted all the way around toward its backside.

"Goddamn thing dragged me all the way over yonder," he said, waving his hand in some vague fashion. "Then these...*shadows* came and...hell, I don't know."

"Hey!" someone called out. Mason Daggett stumbled toward them through a mess of scrub oak. He flopped down on the ground and just shook his head. "Glad to see ya'll...where's my brother?"

"He and Cato...and Greta are back with the wagon," Nina said.

"Nice of ya'll to come looking for us," Strobridge said.

"We ain't looking for you," Nina said, more spite in her voice than she intended. Old enmities die hard sometimes.

Pa cut in and explained the reason for their ill-formed posse.

"Good riddance to that goddamn key," Strobridge spat.

"It's not the fucking key we're after," Nina said, but Father Mathias looked at her sidelong and Manning even turned his head her way a little, too. "Well, some of us are, I suppose. I'm here for Jasmine and Rachel."

Then Mason explained how he'd been snatched up and literally hauled off the ground, found himself soaring through the air in the talons of *something*. When Pa asked him about the critter, he said, "I don't even know. I think I bit its fucking leg off, though."

"You bit it?"

Mason nodded. "Yeah, I bit it, and next thing I know

I'm lying in a patch of that thorny ass bush."

He was a mess for it; part of Mason's earlobe seemed to be missing, there was a hole in his cheek, and his shirt and skin were covered in blood and spiky scrub needles. Nina looked at those talon marks on the man's shoulders. They were deep wounds. She wondered if Mathias would be able to heal them—the priest looked as if he were ready to pitch over any moment.

Red Thunder had gone a ways ahead as they conversed, and he came walking back in the company of Buck Patterson. The roughrider walked right up with a damn unlit cigarette between his lips. "Any matches?" he asked.

Surprisingly, Manning had a couple in his coat, and a couple seconds later he and Buck were passing the quirley back and forth.

No one asked Buck what happened otherwise, and he wasn't telling.

"Let me see that," Nina said and James handed it over. She took a deep draw and suppressed a cough before starting to hand it back.

"If you don't mind?" Mason asked, grimacing as he got up off the ground.

Nina looked at Buck and Buck nodded. She handed it over and Mason inhaled, blew smoke out and sighed, then handed it to Strobridge. Everyone had a puff but Red Thunder took a draw, even her pa, then they set off, though Mason said, "I gotta check on my brother."

No one blamed him for it, and Mason set off back toward the wagon.

Red led the rest of them up a short grade, then through a gulch along the base of a hill. At the end, he stopped and pointed up the rise.

Even Nina could see as much, two sets of tracks were visible in the sodden ground. *What the hell is she doing?*

Red went first, plodding up the steepening rise, turning across its face when necessary, moving in an indirect route to the top. Nina went second and the rest followed behind her. It never got so steep that it presented any real difficulty, though it did take a bit more air in the lungs after the day's tribulations.

Nina caught sight of Jasmine on a rocky precipice, a good fifty feet of air between her and the ground below. Trapped. The Taiping Jing key hung around her neck on a long silver chain.

And she held a knife to Rachel's throat.

Nina wanted to say lots of things. Mainly to tell her to quit mucking about, to come on and let's go. Let's get somewhere safe. But the look in Jasmine's eyes…she was too far gone, a *sure* kind of demented, like she was downright brainsick.

"Why, Jasmine?"

The black woman couldn't meet Nina's gaze at first. She sweated and stammered, looked left and right as if frightened by things that weren't there. After a colossal struggle, she finally met Nina's stare. Her eyes were full of fear and pain.

"I'm sorry, Nina. I didn't mean for this to happen. I didn't mean to take this thing." She plucked at the key hanging from her neck, then put her hand on the back of her head and rubbed it as if working out a pain. "But he been talkin' to me. Come to me in my dreams last night. Not long after I got scratched."

Nina's stomach dropped. "What'd he say, Jaz?"

"He told me if I just brought him this, he'd let ya'll go. He said he wouldn't chase ya'll no more."

"Ya'll? What's that mean?"

Jasmine sobbed. "I'm goin', Nina. With *him*. He promised me...promised me I'd live forever. Promised me all sorts of things I ain't never had."

Pa stepped forward, a gust of wind whipping up strands of his gray-streaked hair. "Hold on. Think about that for a minute. Think about who it is you're dealin' with. This bastard's been chasin' us the better part of a week. He won't think twice about cuttin' your throat once he has that key." Pa drew a slow breath, frustration coloring his cheeks. "You can't deal fair with a demon like Liao. Tell her, Father..."

Mathias blinked up at Jasmine and simply nodded his head. *Damn if our priest ain't sick, too,* Nina thought.

Nina put herself in front of them. Jasmine needed to see her now. A friend. Not men. "It's gonna be *okay*, Jaz. Things are different now. I got my spirit guide. I can help protect us now..."

"No..." Jasmine shook her head feverishly, pressed the blade to Rachel's neck.

The girl screamed, "Jasmine, please!"

Nina watched a thin stream of blood where the girl'd been nicked.

"No, but I'm happy you found your people." Jasmine's sickly face streamed tears. "But they ain't *my* people. I ain't never had no people. It's too late, Nina. Too late. I'm done marked."

"But, Jaz—"

"No," the black girl growled, started to say more, but

stopped. Her face jerked up. Her lip trembled with terror, eyes reflecting something massive moving behind them.

"Let the girl go," Pa hollered.

Nina ducked as a *whoosh* pounded her ears from above; powerful beating wings almost knocked her to the ground.

"Sonofabitch!" Manning cussed, his hand steadying her.

Jasmine cried out in mercy or pain, Nina couldn't tell which, but by the time she looked up, the thing had Jasmine by the shoulders—her arms spread painfully wide—and lifted her into the sky with long, lazy wing beats. Rachel fell to the ground and lay there.

Nina heard a rustle of material, the cock of a pistol. She reached out with her right hand and pushed Manning's dragoon aside. "I've got this."

Nina walked to the precipice and drew her Colt. Cocked it. She gritted her teeth against tears, pointed the barrel, and squeezed off a round.

Missed.

Jasmine stopped struggling, a look of hurt burning across the growing distance. Jasmine's trembling lips mouthed, "Why?"

Nina shot again and again, missing both times.

I can't even shoot her, Nina thought. Jasmine's eyes lit up with hope, even when Nina raised her gun for one last shot. One last bullet was all she had.

The pistol cracked. But it wasn't Nina's gun that went off.

Jasmine jerked as a spot of darker red blossomed on her blouse. Her mouth worked silently, her lungs too mangled to push air. She squirmed in the grasp of the tenuous claws, unable to cover the wound with her arms bound by those wicked talons.

Nina glanced down at Rachel standing on the precipice. She held a small derringer-type pistol, still pointing it up, a small cloud of gunsmoke melting around her. Her shoulders trembled as she wept.

Finally, Jasmine gave up, gazed across the gap. Nina held her gaze until she drew her last breath, and then her friend went still.

CHAPTER SEVENTEEN

GEORGE DAGGETT SCREAMED INTO the rag they'd stuffed into his mouth. He bucked against Mason, Manning, Buck, and Red, all four men holding him down, each to a limb. George lifted them off the floor with his sudden, violent outbursts, getting loose more often than not to deliver a wild kick or punch.

"Damn stronger than he looks," Buck said, his nose bleeding from George's boot heel. "We're even now, son."

"Hold him steady, if you please," Father Mathias told them, sweat dripping down his face. A droplet fell from the tip of his long nose. "I'm going to cut now."

There was a moment's pause, then George Daggett

nearly came up off the table. A high, flatulent whistle breathed into the room, followed by a pungent smell.

In the corner of the room, Rachel wrinkled her nose, and Nina considered the girl and her startling resilience...

She thought back to earlier that day; as the menfolk appropriated room and board at the St. Charles Hotel and took George upstairs, she and Rachel had planted themselves at a small table by one of the building's corner windows. They had sipped their coffee and shared the silence of two sleep-bereft, hard-pressed missies. They hadn't spoken of the incident on the hill the day before; in fact, Rachel hadn't said much at all.

After another sip though, the girl wrinkled her nose at the bitter taste. "Ma was the one who taught me. She was a pretty fair shot, like she told you, but she said I seemed to have a real eye for my target." She smiled. "Daddy couldn't hit the broadside of a barn, though."

Nina returned the smile, tinged with a bit of sadness and fatigue. "If I haven't said it up 'til now, I'm sorry about your family," Nina told her.

Rachel nodded and stared at the steam rising from her mug. "Thanks. I miss them. I miss Jaz, too." She wiped tears away before they could get started.

"So how long you had that gun?"

"I found it on the train, after we crashed. Kept it squirrelled away, kind of as a last resort, you know? For myself. Never dreamed I'd have to use it on a friend." She took a small sip, then stared at the window at the activity on the streets of Carson City.

It was a booming town due to *wasichu* obsession with Gold Hill and the Comstock Lode—that much Nina knew.

Mills and miners dotted the Eagle and Washoe Valleys between here and Virginia City, and on up into Reno. She imagined Strobridge's superiors will be surveying the territory before long. That is if Liao Xu's new world doesn't lay claim to everything first.

Carson City's streets were jammed with bustle morning, noon, and night. Folks going about their business as if the end of the world was *not* on their doorstep. Nina envied their ignorance, their only concerns were where to pan, where to dig, and what saloon was serving nickel shots today.

"There's Mister Strobridge," Rachel said, nodding out the window.

Nina looked out and saw the railroad boss coming off the boardwalk cattycorner from the hotel, a building with signage reading *Overland Telegraph*. He was in the company of several white men—three hard-lookin' fellers trailed behind him, and an older gentleman in a suit walked alongside. She watched Strobridge speak with the gent, who ended up getting red faced and walking away in a huff. Seems the boss man had that effect on most folk.

Strobridge then came inside the St. Charles with his three toughs in tow and hailed the proprietor, a Mister Muller, who had been horrified earlier by their ghastly appearance—though they'd managed to wash down some at a watering hole along the way. Nina could only imagine the reception they would've got waltzing into town covered hat to boot in dried blood and crusty bits of bone and brain all over.

"Injuns," was all the explanation Strobridge provided Mister Muller, as if that one word explained all. The proprietor could wonder about Red Thunder all he wanted, but it seemed none of them gave a good goddamn at this point, and he was gracious enough not to ask.

Right before they'd all headed upstairs to their rooms, Rachel reached across the table and took hold of Nina's hand. "Here," the girl had said, and put the Taiping Jing key in Nina's palm.

"Sakes alive, Rachel! Where'd you get this? We thought we'd lost it."

"Like I said, I keep stuff squirrelled away. I wear my dresses with lots of pockets."

Nina looked at the key, still wrapped with the girl's hair. She closed her fist around it.

"This coffee...*blech*...wretched stuff..." Rachel pushed the mug away and looked up. "I grabbed the key right before Jaz got taken up." She shrugged. "I figure it's important."

"You figured right."

"It's up to you if you want to tell the others. I won't say nothing."

Nina nodded and stowed the key, then she and Rachel followed the men upstairs; all of them except Strobridge and his men who sat at a table, ordered drinks, and started talking business or some such. Didn't matter. At least he'd bought the rooms, saying it was the least he could do.

It stuck in her craw to know her board was on that man's dime, but damn if she weren't looking forward to a hot bath, some chow, and perchance a little private time with James Manning to do things he'd be ashamed to tell the Devil.

But first, there was more business to tend to—Daggett business.

Gᴇᴏʀɢᴇ ᴄᴀᴍᴇ ᴜᴘ ᴀɢᴀɪɴ, this time spitting the rag out of his mouth and sounding off pretty good before Pa stuffed it back in. They pushed him back down.

"Jesus!" Mason took a breath, looking pale. The stitches in his cheek pulling taut. "It's done burrowed into his skull."

George squealed into the rag.

"Indeed," Father Mathias said, clearing his throat and taking on a stronger tenor, as if getting ready to preach the Word—which he was. "Hear me, demon. *Dead* thing. Defiler of the hearts and minds of men. The Lord sent his only son to this Earth to rid it of your kind many hundreds of years ago. It was the Lord Jesus who threw the demons and sinners from his temple, and it is He who commands you. Come out now and face judgment."

A low, tired whine emanated from George Daggett's head. The man's eyes rolled and he passed out.

"I've got most of it," the priest said, working a small tong-like instrument. "Just have to extricate the head."

"Hurry, dammit," Mason said. "He's dying."

"I hope it ain't looking for brains in there. Not a damn thing to eat," Manning said.

Buck laughed softly into his bloody mustache. Mason glared at Manning. "After this, you and me's having words."

"Just trying to keep things light."

"Quit trying."

Manning nodded. "Fair enough."

"Shhh!" Mathias shushed them.

Nina gave Rachel a look. "He and Jaz both said they was scratched." She looked down at her arms where dozens of scabrous red nail marks marred her skin, most of 'em from where deaduns had grabbed hold of her, or at least tried to.

"That's right." Rachel nodded.

"Demon!" Mathias had his Bible resting on George's chest. "Unhold this faithful servant of the Lord, aye, faithful! Let this man, George Daggett, return to the Lord's bosom safe from harm, free from this abominable curse."

"You got it, Father," Pa encouraged.

There was a wet *pop*, and Mathias raised a squirming, gray worm into the air, like some kind of glorious birth. Impossibly fat as a whiskey bottle, it twisted in his hand and nearly fell to the floor. Pa rushed in and took hold of the tail.

"Holy…that was in his head?" Buck gawped at the nasty thing. They all did.

Nina touched the Taiping Jing key in her shirt pocket. It tingled with energy but, still bound against Liao Xu's eyes, was devoid of warmth.

The critter turned and twisted violently, causing Mathias and Pa to stumble into the nightstand. Red Thunder reached out for them, but the two men fell onto the bed, on top of the comatose George, their legs kicking as they still struggled to hold the thing.

"Squeeze it, Lincoln!"

"I got it. Now what?"

"Boot-stomp the fucking thing!" Mason yelled, leaning over his brother's head for protection. George wasn't moving, his jaw open slack, and Nina thought he looked awful dead.

Meantime, Pa and Mathias looked at one another. The priest nodded. "Good idea."

"Okay. One, two, three, *now!*"

There was a wet smack as the critter hit the floor,

just before three boots came down, one after the other, pounding the diabolical larvae into a squashy mess.

"Yuck," Rachel said.

"No kidding," Buck agreed, shaking sludge off his boot. Some of it slopped against the door.

Nina reckoned the folks downstairs must be imagining all sorts of things. What would they think when deadun juice oozed between the floorboards to drip in their potato soup?

"Well done, Father," Pa said, giving Mathias a pat on the back. "It's a baby worm."

"Can ya'll quit making jokes? George don't look so good," Mason snapped.

"Let's see to him. I believe I've got enough left in me to give your brother a fighting chance."

"You got yourself on my good side, Padre, but if my brother dies, I recommend ya'll get out of my sight."

"Noted." Mathias knelt at the bedside and took up his crucifix. "Why don't some of you go wash up and eat? This will take a few minutes, I believe." He laid his right hand on George's forehead. The priest began whispering prayers and shut his eyes.

A minute passed, then two, and the priest continued to pray. Buck and Red filed out first, and Nina saw Cato, garbed in patched overalls and fresh bandages, standing in the hallway leaning against the far wall. Mason, being a contentious Confederate type, had refused to let the black man into the room.

"He alive?" Cato asked, looking genuinely concerned.

Buck grunted something in response, and they filed out of view toward the way downstairs.

"Why don't ya'll join 'em?" Pa said to Nina and Rachel as he pulled a chair to the foot of George's bed and sat in it.

"You sure, Lincoln?" Manning asked. "I don't mind staying."

"No, you go. I'll grab a bite in a few."

"I'll come back up soon as I'm done."

Rachel went with Manning, and Nina said she'd be along shortly. She was distracted, peering out the window.

The crowds were on the move, everyone going someplace or doing something, heading in and out of storefronts, while horses and wagons moved to and fro. Small bunches of folk greeting, yammering, laughing, bidding adios. All of 'em up to some sort of cosmopolitan business.

All except one.

A lone figure stood on the sidewalk, across the street. A figure she hadn't noticed before, but now had caught her full attention. The lady had shoulder-length, black hair, cut in a straight line across her brow, hips and legs shapely beneath a dress of faded deerskin, sun-browned arms bare, with eyes black and lifeless as a winter storm on a dark night. The woman's lips were gray and frosted, as if brushed with ice.

It knew her, and she it.

It will bring you pain.

I can handle pain.

Nina felt the first pangs of it; a heavy pull on her heart, a sort of spiritual dread. The sense that nothing would ever be perfect again.

She put her fingers up to the window pane.

"Hi, Ma."

ABOUT THE AUTHORS

Tim Marquitz

Raised on a diet of Heavy Metal and bad intentions, Tim Marquitz writes a mix of the dark perverse, the horrific, and the tragic, tinged with sarcasm and biting humor. A former grave digger, bouncer, and dedicated metalhead, he is a huge fan of Mixed Martial Arts, and fighting in general. His urban fantasy series called Demon Squad is a fan favorite and he is also the Editor-In-Chief of Ragnarok Publications. He lives in El Paso, Texas, with his beautiful wife and daughter. His website is www.tmarquitz.com.

J.M. Martin

J.M. Martin has been a teacher, an occupational therapist, a managing editor, and a graphic designer. He has written comic books and role-playing games, as well

as several short stories for Fantasist Enterprises, Rogue Blades Entertainment, Pill Hill Press, and Angelic Knight Press. He recently co-founded Ragnarok Publications with Tim Marquitz and is the company's Creative Director. J.M. (Joe) lives in Crestview Hills, Kentucky, with his kick-ass, red-headed, black belt wife and three spirited wee folk he swears are pixies.

Kenny Soward

Kenny Soward grew up in Crescent Park, Kentucky, a small suburb just south of Cincinnati, Ohio, listening to AC/DC, Quiet Riot, and Iron Maiden. In those quiet 1970's streets, he jumped bikes, played Nerf football, and acquired many a childhood scar. At the age of sixteen, he learned to play drums and bashed skins for many groups over the next twenty years. By day, Kenny works as a Unix professional, and at night he writes and sips bourbon. His fantasy series GnomeSaga is published by Ragnarok Publications. He lives in Independence, Kentucky, with two cats and a gal who thinks she's a cat. Visit him online at www.kennysoward.com.

Dead West continues this Fall, 2014, with
THE DEVILS IN RENO

THANKS TO THE RAGNAROK staff and to the Official Street Team. Thanks, as well, to test readers Ron Ruger and Frank Errington for their keen perceptual skills. Thank you, photographer Allen Freeman, and models Shea Dameron, Kinsey Renshaw, and Dean Homsher.

Also we wish to thank fellow publishers Katie Cord and Evil Girlfriend Media, George Cotronis's Kraken Press, and J.L. Murray's Hellzapoppin Press, and the following fantastic authors for taking part in helping promote *The Ten Thousand Things*: Django Wexler, Timothy W. Long, Gini Koch, Eloise J. Knapp, Mercedes M. Yardley, Clint Lee Werner, Rhiannon Frater, Kane Gilmour, and Edward M. Erdelac. Please check out their works! They are fantastic, talented folks.

If you enjoyed *The Ten Thousand Things*, we urge you to post a review, even if it's a couple short sentences, on sites like Amazon and Goodreads. Tell us—and others—what you thought! Studies show peer reviews are the most effective forms of advertising, especially for books from independent publishers; plus, connecting with our readers is always exciting and inspiring.

We are having such a blast with this series. We hope you are, too, and that you'll join us for book three of Dead West, *The Devils in Reno*, coming this Fall, 2014.

For more information about the Dead West series, visit RagnarokPub.com

THANK YOU...

...for purchasing this book!

Visit our website to see more:
Speculative Fiction
Dark Fantasy
Urban Fantasy
Supernatural Horror
Short Story Collections

Please post reviews at online stores and review sites.
Reader Reviews Make a Difference!

www.ragnarokpub.com

www.ingramcontent.com/pod-product-compliance
Lightning Source LLC
Chambersburg PA
CBHW031715170626
46808CB00005B/1762